"Jett," Muirinn c [...]
name? Your son [...]

A raw and wild emotion tore through him. Part of him didn't want to give the name up to her, give anything to her. "Troy," he said quietly.

She was dead silent for a long moment. "My father's name."

"Your father was a good man, Muirinn. I'm proud to use his name for my son."

"I… It just surprises me," Muirinn said quietly.

"It's not for you. It's for a man who knew honor, knew his home. Knew how not to purposefully hurt the people who cared for him."

She stared at him. "Do you really hate me that much?"

"I hate what you did, Muirinn, to the people who loved you."

He walked out and closed the heavy oak door behind him with a soft thud that seemed to shudder down to her bones. She slumped into a chair at the kitchen table and buried her face in her hands.

Dear Reader,

How far would you go to keep a secret? Are some secrets better left buried, or does truth liberate, always? And at what point, exactly, does a secret between two people who care for each other start becoming a lie by omission?

These are questions my heroine, Muirinn O'Donnell, must confront when she returns to her childhood home, where the secret of her father's murder—and her grandfather's death—lies buried deep in an abandoned mine, and in the psyche of a small Alaskan coastal town.

To find the truth she has no choice but to turn to Jett Rutledge, the man she has always loved, but couldn't have. And in unearthing the dark and terrible truths of their shared past, Muirinn and Jett must in turn reveal their own deep secrets—secrets that both bind and divide—and fight for a second chance.

But will a killer give them time?

Loreth Anne White

LORETH ANNE WHITE

Cold Case Affair

Silhouette®
Romantic
SUSPENSE

 SILHOUETTE BOOKS

Recycling programs for this product may not exist in your area.

ISBN-13: 978-0-373-27652-3

COLD CASE AFFAIR

Copyright © 2009 by Loreth Beswetherick

Visit Silhouette Books at www.eHarlequin.com

Printed in U.S.A.

Books by Loreth Anne White

Silhouette Romantic Suspense

*Shadow Soldiers
†Love In 60 Seconds
**Wild Country

LORETH ANNE WHITE

Loreth Anne White was born and raised in southern Africa, but now lives in Whistler, a ski resort in the moody British Columbian Coast Mountain range. It's a place of vast wilderness, larger-than-life characters, epic adventure, and romance—the perfect place to escape reality. It's no wonder she was inspired to abandon a sixteen-year career as a journalist to escape into a world of romantic fiction filled with dangerous men and adventurous women.

When she's not writing you will find her long-distance running, biking or skiing on the trails, and generally trying to avoid the bears—albeit not very successfully. She calls this work, because it's when the best ideas come.

For a peek into her world visit her Web site, www.lorethannewhite.com. She'd love to hear from you.

For Toni Anderson, who is always ready to meet me at the water cooler on days both good and bad.

To Susan Litman, for keeping that bar raised.

And to Jennifer Jackson for believing in me.

Prologue

Seven hundred fifty feet under the Alaskan earth the air was dank, the shaft black as pitch.

Spring runoff—an icy sludge of water and mud—gushed down over him as he descended a wooden ladder slick with rot and moisture, foot by tortuous foot, into the cold womb of the earth. The small lamp on his mining cap pierced the blackness with a quavering halo of yellow, shadows lunging at him whenever he moved.

It was 3:42 a.m.

By the time he reached the 800 level, his knee was locked in pain, his fingers dead. He suffered from *white hand*—the nerves in his hands permanently damaged from the constant vibration of the heavy pneumatic jackleg drill that shuddered daily through his body as he drove blast holes into rock.

Miners got cold, they got wet and they got old as they toiled in perpetual blackness, forcing tunnels deeper and deeper into the bowels of the earth to extract ore that would be turned into bright, gleaming gold. And he was no different—his body just as battered.

Dragging his left leg now, he made his way to the scoop tram shop. He was edgy. Even at this hour, someone could be in this part of the mine. He took a tram and drove it along the tunnel to the powder magazine. Breathing hard, he worked quickly to load two bags of explosives, a couple of powder sticks, detonator caps, B-line.

By 5:02 a.m. he was tackling the knee-grinding, lung-busting seventy-story ascent to the earth's surface. He exited the shaft at the deserted Sodwana headframe, three miles away from the main gates of the Tolkin Mine, limbs shaking. Waiting for him in cold predawn shadows was a friend with a hard shot of whiskey and a ride back into town.

At 6:33 a.m., on that bleak Alaskan morning, a man-car loaded with twelve miners trundled and screeched along the black drift eight hundred feet below ground. The men—all from the small town of Safe Harbor—huddled facing each other, knees touching, clutching thermoses and lunch pails as they made their way to their workstations for the day.

The beam from the headlamp of the man sitting in front lit the rail ahead. He spun around suddenly, terror on his face as he tried to shout a warning.

But it was too late.

The blast was massive, rocking the ground above, registering on sensitive seismic monitoring equipment as far away as the university in Anchorage.

The first external agency to be notified of an unexplained explosion in the bowels of Tolkin Mine was the Safe Harbor Fire Department. Seconds later Safe Harbor Hospital was on high alert for possible mass casualties, and frantic calls were going out for all available doctors to be on standby. These calls were picked up on home scanners, the news rippling like brushfire through the small, close-knit community. Family members hysterical with worry converged on the mine site.

Adam Rutledge, head of mine rescue and the shop steward for the local miners' union, scrambled into his Draegers—mine rescue gear complete with breathing apparatus. He hurriedly contacted the members of his volunteer team.

When they reached the mine, acrid black smoke was billowing out from D-shaft and the extraction vents. At this point, no one aboveground knew what had happened eight hundred feet below. Snowflakes began to crystallize in the frigid air and a group of women shivered together against a biting wind, not knowing if their men were alive, injured or dead.

Among them was Mary O'Donnell, clutching the hand of her nine-year-old daughter, Muirinn.

Muirinn watched the rescuers tumble out of a bright yellow bus in their Draegers, led by their neighbor, Adam Rutledge—her friend Jett's father.

But a police officer flanked by burly mine security men stopped Adam and his crew at the gate. One had a gun. Angry voices carried on snatches of wind as Adam clashed with the police. A German shepherd strained against his leash, barking and baring teeth at Adam. The cop then drew his gun. Adam raised both hands, backing off. Swearing.

Muirinn grew very scared.

She knew the whole town was at war over the big mine strike, neighbors pitted against neighbors, family members against each other. That's why all the police and security men were here. Still, she didn't understand why they wouldn't let Mr. Rutledge and the mine rescue team in—her *dad* was down there.

Desperation squeezed the nine-year-old's heart.

Snow swirled thicker. Temperatures dropped.

Slowly, miners began to emerge from the earth, blackened with soot, choking from emergency stench gas released by management into the tunnels to warn them out of the mine. Muirinn and her mother stood alone as other families were reunited all around them. A few women started to sob. Their men hadn't come up yet, either.

Then Safe Harbor Police Chief Bill Moran came striding through the snow toward Muirinn and her mother, flakes settling thick on the wide brim of his hat.

When she saw the look in his eyes, Muirinn knew her daddy was never coming back.

By late afternoon, Chief Moran had examined the scene and learned of the two bags of explosives missing from the powder magazine. Positive he was now dealing with a mass homicide investigation, he'd contacted the FBI field office in Anchorage, and Tolkin Mine was locked down as they waited for the post-blast team. But the spring snowstorm had other ideas. It barreled in and powered down with a vengeance, unleashing blizzard-force winds on Safe Harbor, cutting off access to the remote Alaskan coastal community. The FBI team was unable to land in Safe Harbor for a full forty-eight hours. The television crews came shortly after, filling the few hotels and restaurants in the tiny mining town. As the story of mass murder in the North broke, it rippled across television screens south of the 49th.

Three months later, Muirinn stood beside a hospital bed, tears streaming down her face. Sheer grief had stolen her mother's life.

Muirinn was taken home to be raised by her grandfather, Gus O'Donnell, her last living relative.

Someone had planted a bomb that had killed Muirinn's father, taken her mother, and changed her life forever.

And the police never found him.

The heinous secret remained buried deep in the abandoned black tunnels of Tolkin Mine. And a mass murderer still walked among the villagers of Safe Harbor.

Chapter 1

Twenty years later

The wings banked as the pilot began a steep descent into an amphitheater of shimmering glacial peaks at the head of Safe Harbor Inlet, a small and isolated community that clung to a rugged coastline hundreds of miles west of Anchorage.

When Muirinn O'Donnell fled this place eleven years ago, those granite mountains had been a barrier to the rest of the world, a rock and ice prison she'd sought desperately to escape. Now they were simply beautiful.

Pontoons slapped water, and the tiny yellow plane squatted down into a churning white froth as the engines slowed to a growl. The pilot taxied toward a bobbing float plane dock.

She was back, the prodigal daughter returned—almost seven months' pregnant, and feeling so incredibly alone.

Muirinn clasped the tiny whalebone compass on a small chain around her neck, drawing comfort from the way it warmed against her palm. Her grandfather, Gus O'Donnell, had left her the small compass, along with everything else he owned, including the house at Mermaid's Cove and Safe Harbor Publishing, his newspaper business.

His death had come as a terrible shock.

Muirinn had been on assignment in the remote jungles of West Papua for the magazine *Wild Spaces* when Gus's body had been found down a shaft at the abandoned Tolkin Mine, a full thirteen days after he'd first been reported missing. And no one had been able to reach her until two weeks ago.

She'd missed his cremation and the memorial service, and she was having trouble wrapping her head around the circumstances of his death.

Muirinn had called the medical examiner herself. He'd told her Gus had been treated for years for a heart condition, and that he'd suffered cardiac arrest while down the mine shaft, which had apparently caused him to tumble a short way from the ladder to the ground. Muirinn could not imagine why her eccentric old grandfather would have been alone in the shaft of an abandoned mine. *Especially* if he had heart trouble.

And she was unable to accept that the dank maw of Tolkin had swallowed the life of someone else she loved.

Gus had raised her solo from the age of nine, after the death of her parents, and while Muirinn had never come home to visit him, she'd loved her grandfather beyond words.

Just the knowledge that Gus was in this world had made her feel part of something larger, a family. In losing Gus, she'd somehow lost her roots.

All she had now was this little compass to guide her.

Muirinn peered out the small window as the floatplane approached the dock, thinking that nothing had changed, yet everything had. Then suddenly she saw him.

Jett Rutledge.

The one person she'd sought to avoid for the past eleven years. The reason she'd stayed away from her hometown.

He stood at the ferry dock on the opposite side of the harbor, wearing jeans and a white T-shirt, his skin tanned summer dark, his body lean and strong. His thick blue-black hair glistened in the late-evening sun.

Muirinn's stomach turned to water.

She leaned forward, hand pressing up against the window as the plane swung around and bumped against the dock. And like a hungry voyeur she watched as the man she'd never stopped loving crouched down to talk to a boy—a boy with the same shock of blue-black hair. The same olive-toned complexion.

His son.

Muirinn's eyes brimmed with emotion.

He ruffled the child's hair, put a baseball cap on the boy's head and cocked the peak down over his eyes. Jett stood as his kid raced toward the ferry, little red backpack bobbing against his back.

The child hesitated at the base of the gangplank, drawn by some invisible tie to his father. He spun around suddenly, and even from this distance Muirinn could see the bright slash of a smile in the boy's sun-browned face as he waved fiercely to his dad one last time before boarding the boat.

At the same time a woman approached Jett, the ocean wind toying with strands of her long blond hair. Her stride was confident, happy. She placed her hand on Jett's arm, gave him a kiss, then followed the child up the passenger ramp.

That vignette—framed by the small float plane window— struck Muirinn hard.

Her eyes blurred with emotion and a lump formed in her throat. As the sound of the prop died down and the plane door was swung open, Muirinn heard the ferry horn and saw the boat pulling out into the choppy inlet.

Jett walked slowly to the edge of the dock, hands thrust deep in his jeans pockets as he watched the ferry drawing away in a steady white *V* of foam. He gave one last salute, hand held high in the air, a solitary yet powerful figure on the dock. A lighthouse, a rock to which his boy would return.

"You ready to deplane, ma'am?"

Shocked, she turned to face the pilot. He had a hand held out to her, a look of concern in his eyes. She got that a lot at this stage of her pregnancy.

"Thank you," she said, quickly donning her big, protective sunglasses as she took his hand. She stepped down onto the wooden dock, disoriented after her long series of flights from New York. Two cabs waited up on the road as the handful of passengers from Anchorage disembarked around her.

Muirinn climbed into the first taxi and gave directions to what was now her property on Mermaid's Cove, a small bay tucked into the ragged coastline a few miles north of town. But on second thought she leaned forward. "I'm sorry, but could you take the long way around town? Not along the harbor road."

Or the past the airstrip.

There was a risk of seeing Jett again if they went that way. She wasn't ready for that—even from a distance. Not now.

Not after seeing him with his son. And his wife.

Muirinn's lawyer in New York had told her that Jett Rutledge had led the search team that located Gus's body in the mine. This news had rattled her—the idea of Jett still here in Safe Harbor, still saving people when she hadn't allowed him to save her all those years ago. It was almost too painful to imagine.

Muirinn also knew from her grandfather that Jett had married in Las Vegas shortly after she'd left town eleven years ago, and that he'd had a child. The news had nearly killed her because Jett had refused to follow *her* to Los Angeles just a few months before. And when she'd learned that she was pregnant with Jett's baby, she'd been too proud—too afraid— to return home. And so she'd chosen to bear the child alone.

At nineteen, with no money and few prospects, Muirinn had ended up giving *their* baby up for adoption, a decision that still haunted her.

She'd never gotten over it.

Muirinn had also learned from Gus that Jett had joined the ranks of Alaska's bush pilots, a free-spirited breed unto themselves. And that's when she'd told her grandfather to stop.

She didn't want to hear one more word about Jett and his happy little family. It was driving her crazy with the pain of her own losses, so Muirinn had resorted to her tried-and-true coping mechanism—she just severed ties, cutting herself off from the source of her angst. And her grandfather had respected her request.

From that point on, Muirinn knew nothing more about Jett's life. She hadn't even wanted to know his wife's name. And sheer stubborn pride forbade her from ever asking about Jett again, or from coming home. Pride, and her dark secret.

All Muirinn knew for certain was that she'd lost the only man she'd ever loved through the biggest mistake of her life. One she'd never stopped regretting. Because after Jett she'd had one failed relationship after another, no man ever quite measuring up to him.

Which was why she was having a baby on her own now.

She sank back into the cab seat, wondering where Jett's son and wife were going on that ferry. It was late July. School was out. The kid might be going to a summer camp, or with his mother on a trip to Seattle. Anywhere.

It was none of her business.

Muirinn had given up any claim to Jett Rutledge a long, long time ago.

Yet a poignant sadness pressed through her, and she closed her eyes, placing her hand on her belly.

Do you still hate me so much, Jett?

What would she do if his parents still owned the neighboring property on Mermaid's Cove?

Muirinn had grown up on that cove. She and Jett had stolen their first-ever kiss down in the old boat shed, hidden from the houses by a dense grove of trees. She wondered if the shed still stood.

They'd made love for the first time in that shed, too, on a night the moon had shimmered like silver over the water. She'd just turned eighteen, and Jett twenty-one. The boat shed had become their special place, and there was a time Muirinn had thought it would all be there for her forever.

But the summer she turned nineteen, everything changed.

As the cab neared the Mermaid's Cove property, Muirinn asked the driver to drop her off at the ramshackle gate.

Bags in hand, she stood at the top of the overgrown driveway, staring down at her childhood home as the taxi pulled off in a cloud of soft glacial dust.

The scene in front of her seemed to shimmer up out of her memory to take literal shape in front of her—the garden and forest fighting for supremacy; brooding firs brushing eaves with heavy branches. Wild roses scrambled up the staircase banisters, and berry bushes bubbled up around the wooden deck that ran the length of the rustic log house.

On the deck terra-cotta pots overflowed with flowers,

herbs, vegetables; all evidence of her grandfather's green thumb. And beyond the deck, the lawn rolled down to a grove of trees, below which Mermaid's Cove shimmered.

In a few short months this would all be gone and piled high with snow. Safe Harbor was known for the heaviest accumulation among Alaskan coastal towns.

Numbly, Muirinn walked down the driveway and set her bags at the base of the deck stairs, bending to crush a few rosemary leaves between her fingers as she did.

She drank in the scent of the herbs, listening to the hum of bees, the distant chink of wind chimes, the chuckle of waves against tiny stones in the bay below. It amazed her to think that her grandfather was actually gone; evidence of his life thrummed everywhere.

She looked up at the house, and suddenly felt his presence.

I'm so sorry for not coming home while you were still here. I'm sorry for leaving you alone.

A sudden breeze rippled through the branches, brushing through her hair. Muirinn swallowed, unnerved, as she picked up her bags.

She made her way up the stairs and dug the house key out of her purse.

Pushing open the heavy oak door with its little portal of stained glass, Muirinn stepped into the house, and back into time. She heard his gruff voice almost instantly.

'Tis the sea faeries that brought you here, Muirinn. The undines. They brought you up from the bay to your mother and father, to me. To care for you for all time.

Emotion burned sharply into her eyes as her gaze scanned the living room, full of books, paintings, photos of her and her parents. For years Muirinn hadn't thought of those fantastical tales Gus had spun in her youth. She'd managed to lock those magical myths away deep in the recesses of her memory, behind logic and reason and the practicalities of work and life in a big city. But now they swept over her—there was no holding them back. This homecoming was going to be rougher than she thought.

More than anything, though, it was Gus's artwork that grabbed her by the throat.

She slumped into a chair, staring at the paintings and sketches that graced the walls. She was in almost all of them—images of a wild imp, frozen in time, in charcoal, in soft ethereal watercolor. In some, her hair flowed out in corkscrew curls as she swam in the sea with the tail of a fish. In others, Gus had taken artistic license with her features, giving her green eyes even more of a mischievous upward slant, her ears a slight point, depicting her as one of the little woodland creatures he used to tell her lived up in the hills.

Eccentric to the core, Gus O'Donnell had been just like this place. Rough, yet spiritual. Wise, yet a dreamer. A big-game hunter, fisherman, writer, poet, artist. A lover of life and lore with a white shock of hair, a great bushy beard and the keen eyes of an eagle.

And he'd raised her just as wildly, eclectically, to be free.

Not that it had boded well for her. Because Muirinn hadn't *felt* free. All she'd wanted to do was escape, discover the real world beyond her granite prison.

Sitting there in a bent-willow rocker, staring at her grandfather's things, exhaustion finally claimed Muirinn, and she fell into a deep sleep.

She woke several hours later, stiff, confused. Muirinn checked the clock—it was almost 10:00 p.m. At this latitude, at this time of year, it barely got dark at night. However, clouds had started scudding across the inlet, lowering the dusky Arctic sky with the threat of a thunderstorm. A harsh wind was already swooshing firs against the roof.

Muirinn tried to flick on a light switch before realizing that she had yet to figure out how to reconnect the solar power. She lit an oil lamp instead and climbed the staircase to her grandfather's attic office. The lawyer had said all the keys she'd need for the house, along with instructions on how to connect the power, would be in the middle drawer of her grandfather's old oak desk.

She creaked open the attic door.

Shadows sprang at her from the far corners of the room. Muirinn's pulse quickened.

Her grandfather's carved desk hulked at the back of the room in front of heavy drapes used to block out the midnight sun during the summer months. A candle that had drowned in its own wick rested on the polished desk surface, along with Gus's usual whiskey tumbler. A pang of emotion stung Muirinn's chest.

It was as if the room were still holding its breath, just waiting for Gus to walk back in. And a strong and sudden sense gripped Muirinn that her grandfather had not been ready to quit living.

She shook the surreal notion, and stepped into the room. The attic air stirred softly around her, cobwebs lifting in currents caused by her movement. Muirinn halted suddenly. She could swear she felt a presence. Someone—or something—was in here.

Again Muirinn shook the sensation.

She set the oil lamp on the desk and seated herself in her grandfather's leather chair. It groaned as she leaned forward to pull open the top drawer. But as she did, a thud sounded on the wooden floor, and something brushed against her leg. Muirinn froze.

She almost let out a sob of relief when she saw that it was only Quicksilver, her grandfather's enormous old tomcat with silver fur, gold eyes, and the scars of life etched into his grizzled face. He jumped onto the desk, a purr growling low in his throat.

"Goodness, Quick," she whispered, stroking him. "I didn't see you come in." He responded with an even louder rumble, and Muirinn smiled. Someone had clearly been feeding the old feline since Gus disappeared because Quicksilver was heavy and solid, if ancient.

The lawyer had mentioned that Gus's old tenant, Mrs. Wilkie, still did housekeeping for him. She must've been taking care of the cat, too.

As Muirinn stroked the animal, she felt the knobs in his crooked tail, broken in two places when he'd caught it in the screen door so many years ago. Again, the sense of stolen time overwhelmed her. And with it came the guilt.

Guilt at not once having come home in eleven years.

The cat stepped into the open drawer and Muirinn edged him aside to remove the bunch of keys, her hand stilling as she caught sight of a fat brown envelope. On it was scrawled the word *Tolkin* in Gus's bold hand. Muirinn removed the envelope, opened it.

Inside was a pile of old crime scene photos, most of which Muirinn recognized from a book Gus had written on the tragedy. A chill rippled over her skin.

Had Gus *still* been trying to figure out who'd planted the Tolkin bomb?

Despite the protracted FBI investigation, the mass

homicide had never been solved. Yet while the case had turned old and cold, her grandfather had remained obsessed with it, convinced that his son's killer still lived and walked among them in Safe Harbor.

Clearly, not even writing the bestseller had put his curiosity to rest, thought Muirinn.

She opened the drawer and spotted Gus's laptop tucked at the very back. Her curiosity now piqued, she decided to take the envelope and the laptop downstairs to her old bedroom and look at them in bed. Perhaps she'd learn why her grandfather had gone down into that dark shaft of the abandoned mine, alone.

Jett Rutledge reached forward and turned up the volume of his truck radio. *"I believe in miracles"* blared from the speakers as he drove, arm out the window. In spite of the dark storm rolling in, he felt happier than he had in a long time.

He'd had a hard workout, a good dinner, a few beers with his dad at the airport club, and he'd taken some time off flying. He was now going to use this period when Troy was away at summer camp to focus on his big dream project. He wanted to prepare several more proposals that would secure financing for the next phase of a fishing lodge he was building in the wilderness farther north.

He turned onto the dirt road that snaked down to Mermaid's Cove, heading for home. His parents had ceded their rolling oceanfront property to him years ago, opting to relocate closer to town themselves. His mother still worked occasionally as a nurse at Safe Harbor Hospital, and everything was generally more accessible from the new house—including his dad's physiotherapy.

Few jobs aged a man quite as fast as mining. Especially working a mine like Tolkin.

The ground at Tolkin was solid rock, which meant fewer cave-ins, fewer deaths, but it also meant the company had racked up a disproportionately large number of other injuries related to the kidney and back-jarring stress of high-impact drilling.

A miner's equipment was heavy. The men were constantly wet. Cold. The thunderous din and fumes of diesel equipment were rough on ears and respiratory tracts. And jarring along the drifts in massive trucks took its toll on bodies. So did negotiating the black ground on foot—the tunnel surfaces were invariably booby-trapped with water-filled potholes that wrenched knees, ankles and shredded tendons.

Which was what had happened to Adam Rutledge.

Jett's dad had taken his fair share of a beating, and his injuries were worsening with arthritis and age.

But he was still alive, still watching his grandson grow, and now he was helping out with communications at the airstrip, a job Jett had scored for his father. All in all, Jett couldn't ask for more.

As he neared Gus's place, he wondered what was going to happen to the old man's property now that he was gone. A thought flashed briefly through his mind that he might make an offer, join the Rutledge land with the O'Donnell acreage. But that idea led to thoughts of Muirinn O'Donnell and he instantly quashed the notion. She'd probably inherited the property. Putting in an offer would just bring him into contact with her. Jett figured he'd rather forgo the option of buying it if meant ever seeing, or talking, to her again.

His hands tensed on the wheel, anger flooding into his veins at the mere thought of Muirinn. She hadn't even shown up for Gus's funeral. That told him something.

It told him that she didn't care.

She didn't give a damn about the people she'd left behind

in this town. She'd turned her back on it all—on him—and never once looked back.

Eleven years ago, Muirinn had been doing a summer stint at her grandfather's newspaper where she'd discovered a passion for journalism. Around the same time a Hollywood production company had blown into town to do a movie on the Tolkin Mine murders, based on Gus's book. The presence of the movie crew had turned Safe Harbor upside down, and it had fired a burning coal in Muirinn's belly. She'd started going out to the set every day, reporting on the production, interviewing the actors and crew. In turn, the actor playing the part of Muirinn's father had interviewed Muirinn as the surviving O'Donnell family member. In Jett's opinion it had messed with her head, giving her a false sense of celebrity.

Then one of the crew members had suggested that Muirinn's writing was really good, saying he'd put a word in for her at his sister's Los Angeles magazine, and Muirinn had become completely obsessed by the idea.

Lured by absurd notions of fame, fortune and escape, she'd packed up her life and followed the crew to LA. Jett had literally begged her not to leave. He'd been so in love with that woman. He'd planned to marry her, never a doubt in his mind that they were meant for each other. But she'd been as stubborn as mule.

They'd argued hot and hard, and it had led to even hotter and angrier sex. Afterwards, she'd tried to convince Jett to go with her, but he couldn't. He was born to live in the wilds of Alaska. It would've killed him to move to L.A. She'd taunted him, saying that if he really loved her enough he'd do it. And Jett, feeling her slipping from his grasp, had retaliated by saying if she did leave, he'd never forgive her, never speak to her again. He'd hate her for walking out on what they had.

Clearly, she'd taken him at his word, because the next day she'd boarded that plane and he'd never heard from her again.

Muirinn had always had a way of bringing out the irrational fire in Jett, something he regretted to this day. Because even through all his anger, Jett never had managed to let Muirinn go, and it had cost him his marriage. It had cost *them*... He slammed on the brakes suddenly, on the road just past Gus's house.

A light was flickering faintly up in Gus's attic window. *Someone was inside.*

Vandals? A fire?

He put his truck into reverse, quickly backed up the road and wheeled into the rutted driveway with half a mind to alert the police before deciding it was likely just old Lydia Wilkie in there, probably using an oil lamp since the power had been disconnected after Gus's death.

Still, it was past midnight; not a time the crazy old lady would likely be up and about inside Gus's house.

He'd better check to make sure.

Muirinn's sleep was shattered by a violent clap of thunder.

She jolted upright. Then she heard it again—not thunder— a thunderous banging on the door downstairs. Quicksilver shot off the bed and bolted down the hall.

Muirinn groped in the dark to light the lamp. Holding it high, she negotiated the stairs, careful not to trip over her nightdress. She halted in the hallway, glanced at the old clock. It was past midnight. Who on earth could be beating on Gus's door at this hour?

The banging shuddered through the house again. Fear sliced into her.

She set the lamp down, reached for the bunch of keys she'd left on the hall table before going to bed. Fumbling for the right key, Muirinn headed for Gus's gun cabinet. Another wave of banging resounded through the house.

Unlocking the cabinet, Muirinn removed Gus's old shotgun. Hands shaking now, she loaded a cartridge, chambered the round and went to the door.

"Who is it?" she yelled.

Wind rattled hard at windows, swished through the conifers outside, branches clawing on the roof. Whoever was out there in the storm couldn't hear her, and the pounding began again, so hard the door shook. She sucked in a deep breath and swung the door open.

And froze.

Chapter 2

"*M*uirinn?"

Shock slammed into Jett's chest.

The flame in the old lantern on the hall table quivered in the wind, making shadows dance over her copper hair. But she simply stared at him, green eyes glimmering, her face ghost-white, shotgun pointed at his heart.

Jett's gaze flickered sharply at the sight of her pregnant belly under the white cotton nightdress. "What are you doing here?" His voice came out rough, raw.

Muirinn slowly lowered the 12-gauge, her left hand rising as if to reach out and touch him. Anticipation ripped through him hot and fast. But she pushed a fall of sleep-tangled curls back from her face instead, and he realized that she was shaking. "Jett?" she whispered.

He was speechless.

Nothing in this world could have prepared him for the

sheer physical jolt of seeing Muirinn O'Donnell back in Safe Harbor. Especially barefoot and *pregnant*.

The pulse at her neck was racing, making the small compass on a chain at her throat catch the light. It lured his gaze down to her breasts, which were full and rounded. Lust tore through him, his blood already pounding with adrenaline. Every molecule in his body screamed to touch her, pull her against him, hold her so damn tight, erase the lost years. But at the same time the sight of her softly rounded belly triggered something cold and brittle in him, a protective shell forming around his raw emotions.

He needed to step away, fast, before he did or said something stupid. "I didn't know you were back," he said crisply. "I saw a light up in the attic, thought it might be vandals."

She was still unable to answer, and his words hung like an inane echo in the chasm of lost years between them. Rain began to plop on the deck.

"Gus's place has been empty," he explained further, clearing his throat. "But I can see you have things under control." Jett turned to go, but he hesitated on the stairs, snared by a fierce urge to turn around, drink in the sight of her once again. "Welcome home, Muirinn," he said brusquely, then he ran lightly down the steps toward his truck, forcing himself not to look back.

"Jett—wait!"

He stilled, rain dampening his hair.

"I…I wasn't in the attic," she said.

He turned very slowly. "You weren't up there when I knocked?"

She shook her head. "I was sleeping."

"Someone was up there, Muirinn."

"It wasn't me."

He wavered, then stalked back up the stairs, flicking on the light switch as he entered the house. Nothing happened.

"I haven't figured out how to reconnect the solar power yet."

"Here, give me that," he said, taking the shotgun from her. "I'll go check things out for you, connect the power, then I'll be gone."

He snagged the lantern from the table and thudded up the wooden stairs.

Muirinn pressed her trembling hand to her stomach, trying to collect herself. Then, forcing out a huge breath, she followed him—and the light—up to the attic.

He creaked open the attic door, the movement causing a draft to rush in from the attic window behind Gus's desk. Drapes billowed out, scattering papers to the floor. Outside, the rain fell heavier, the breeze carrying the moisture in with it.

"I...I could swear that window wasn't open earlier," Muirinn said, moving quickly into the study and stooping to gather the documents scattered across the Persian rug. Her movements were awkward around her growing stomach and she could sense Jett watching her. She stilled, and her gaze slid up to meet him.

In the light of her lantern, the planes of his face were rough, utterly masculine. His mouth was shaped with a sculptor's fine precision, wide and bracketed by laugh lines that had deepened over the years. New, too, were the fine creases that fanned out from his cobalt eyes—eyes still as clear and piercing as the day she'd left town. And they bored into her now with an animal-like intensity that turned her knees to jelly.

Muirinn swallowed.

She knew he had to be thinking about her pregnancy. She also knew that he was too damn proud to ask. They were alike in so many ways.

She stood up, awkwardly clutching the papers to her belly, her cheeks flushing as something darkened in his eyes. Something that made her feel dangerously warm inside.

"It must have been how Quicksilver got in," she said quietly, trying to fill the volatile space between them. "My cat," she explained, then laughed nervously. "Gus got him for me when I turned thirteen, remember?"

"That cat can hardly be called yours, Muirinn," he said crisply. "You left him. Eleven years ago."

The implication was clear. She didn't have any rights. Not here, not anymore, not in Jett's eyes. Not even to a cat.

She moistened her lips.

Jett turned from her suddenly and crossed the room. He held the lantern up behind Gus's desk. "You didn't see this, either?"

"God, no!" Muirinn said, coming to his side and seeing shards of glass glinting on the carpet. The desk drawers had been wrenched open, too, folders lying scattered beneath the leather chair in which she'd sat only hours before. The computer tower beneath the desk was toppled onto its side, wires ripped from the back. A chill rustled through her.

"Someone was up here, Jett, while I was sleeping."

Jett yanked back the heavy drapes. "The windowpane's been shattered. Whoever came in here must have ransacked Gus's desk." He frowned, surveying the scene. "The sound of my truck must have interrupted them."

Muirinn wrapped her arms over her tummy, shivering as the rain-damp wind from the broken window whispered over her skin. "Why would someone want to go through Gus's things?"

"Hell knows," he said, studying the floorboards under the window. "But whoever did this was clearly looking for something. He might've tried to take the whole computer tower because your solar power is off, and he couldn't access the information he wanted right here."

"He?"

"There's dirt transfer on the wooden floor here, left by a boot, about a size 12. I'd say it was a guy."

Another gust of wind chased a ripple of goose bumps over her skin, tightening her nipples. Jett glanced at her breasts, then caught her eyes for a long beat. He looked away quickly, rubbing his brow as he cursed softly.

"Is it that hard, Jett?" she whispered. "Seeing me again?"

He kept his face turned away from her for a long moment.

"Yeah," he mumbled. "It is. Come—" He touched her elbow, gently ushering her out onto the landing. "We should leave the scene as is. I'll call the cops."

He pulled the attic door closed behind them, the space on the narrow landing suddenly close, the halo of lantern light too intimate. Jett had that effect on space—it shrank around him. It wasn't just his physical size; he radiated a kinetic energy that simply felt too large for contained spaces. He thrived out in the wilderness, and it was why he'd refused to follow her to Los Angeles. He'd said the city would kill his spirit, who he was.

In retrospect, Muirinn knew he was right. A crowded urban environment wouldn't accommodate a man with a latent wildness like Jett's. He was born to roam places like Alaska, the tundra, in his plane. It's why people like him came north of 60 in the first place.

Los Angeles would have been a concrete prison for him. But at the time, it had represented freedom and adventure to her—a key to a vibrant new world.

Yet, he *had* left for a while. He'd gone to Las Vegas. Where he'd gotten married. And that *really* burned.

It also made him a hypocrite.

He glanced down into her eyes, sensuality swimming into his features.

"Jett—" she said quietly.

He swallowed, tension growing thicker. "Get something warm on, Muirinn," he said abruptly. "I'm going to call this in. Then I'll connect your power and wait with you until someone from the police department arrives."

She blew out a shaky breath, nodded. "Thanks for doing this."

He held her eyes a moment longer, then jogged down the stairs without a word.

Jett stood in the brick archway, quietly watching Muirinn busying herself in Gus's rustic, open-plan kitchen. She'd pulled one of her grandfather's voluminous sweaters over her white nightgown, and she'd caught her rampant copper curls back in a barrette. He felt relieved—the other look was driving him to total distraction…or destruction. Same difference with Muirinn O'Donnell.

Damn if he hadn't gone red-hot at the sight of her on hands and knees in that cotton nightgown as she'd gathered up Gus's papers, strewn all over the attic office. There was something about her pregnant body that drove him wild. And made him incredibly sad.

Hurt.

She'd always had such power over him, yet she'd never known the extent of her control. But now, in Gus's oversized sweater, she looked small, vulnerable. Jett wasn't so sure this look was any better for his health. It aroused protective instincts in him—things he didn't want to feel for her. This was such a total shock, seeing her again, without warning. He needed to figure out what this might mean to his family. To his son.

To him.

"Hey," she said with a soft smile, as she caught him watching. His blood quickened.

He stepped into the kitchen, making sure he remained on the opposite side of the rough wood table.

She poured him tea from a stubby copper kettle, which she set back on the gas stove, still steaming. He avoided eye contact as he took a seat at the table, and accepted the mug from her.

She'd made his tea just the way he liked it, black and sweet. The fact that she even remembered cut way too close to the bone. Why *should* it matter? Truth was, it did.

Everything about Muirinn mattered.

And right now he was struggling with his emotions, trying to avoid the elephant in the room that was her pregnancy, trying to be the gentleman and not ask, yet desperate to know who the father was, where he was. Why she was here alone.

The fact that she was expecting a baby at all sliced Jett like a knife. He forced out a heavy breath of air. Civility be damned—they were beyond that. There was no way to be polite about what had transpired between them, no way to bridge the divide with small talk. So he chose a direct approach. "You never came to visit Gus," he said quietly. "You didn't even come home for the funeral. So why are you here now?"

She studied him with those shrewd cat eyes for a moment. "I came to take over Safe Harbor Publishing, Jett. Gus left me the company in his will, along with this property."

He literally felt himself blanch. "You're going to *stay?*"

Pain flickered over her features. "Maybe." She inhaled deeply, bracing her hands on the back of a chair. "The will stipulated that I could sell the business, but only after a year. That means running it myself for twelve months, or hiring someone else to do it."

"So you're here to hire someone?"

"No. I'm here to run it."

"For one year?"

"Look, Jett, I'm not going to get in your way, okay? I'm not going to cramp your style." She hesitated. "I...I saw you down at the ferry dock this morning, with your son—" She wavered again, as if not quite trusting herself to say the next words. "And your wife."

Perspiration prickled across his lip. He'd made a mistake starting this conversation now. He set the mug down, getting up in the same movement, and he stalked into the hall. "I'll just go wait outside for Officer Gage."

"Jett?" she called after him.

He halted, hand on the doorknob.

"What's his name? Your son?"

A strange emotion tore through him, raw and wild. Part of him didn't want to give the name up to her, give any part of *his* boy to her. "Troy," he said quietly, still facing the door. "Troy Rutledge."

She was dead silent for a long moment. "Troy was my father's name."

"Your father was a good man, Muirinn. I was proud to name my son after him."

"I...it just surprises me."

He turned. "Why?"

"Half the town—the union hardliners—*hated* my dad for crossing that picket line, your own father included. They called my dad a scab, called me terrible names at school, humiliated my mother in the supermarket. They hated my father enough to blow him and eleven others up with a bomb."

"It was a bad time for everyone, Muirinn." Jett paused. "But no matter what people said, you know that I always cared for your father. If Troy O'Donnell hadn't introduced me to model airplanes, to the idea of flying, I might have become a miner, not a pilot. He was the one who told me, when I was ten years old, that I could do something better with my life than go down that mine. He was a friend, Muirinn. I was twelve when he died, and I was also devastated by his murder. It ate my father up, too, regardless of what he might have said about your dad."

Emotion seeped into her eyes, making her nose pink— making her so damn beautiful. "Thank you, Jett," she whispered. "I...I needed to hear that."

"It's not for you," he said quietly. "It's for a man who knew honor, knew his home. Knew how not to deliberately hurt the people who cared for him."

She stared at him. "Do you really still hate me that much?"

Wind rattled the panes. Rain smacked at the windows. "I hate what you did, Muirinn, to the people who loved you."

He closed the heavy oak door behind him with a soft thud that seemed to resonate down through her bones.

Muirinn slumped into a chair at the kitchen table, and buried her face in her hands. If she'd known it was going to be quite so rough to see him again, she wouldn't have come. If Jett only knew what she'd gone through since she'd left Safe Harbor. He didn't have a clue just how much his ultimatum had cost her back then...how much it had cost *them*.

She should've told the lawyer to just go ahead and hire someone—anyone—to run Safe Harbor Publishing, and to put the word out that the company would be up for grabs within twelve months.

But at the same time, Muirinn felt in her heart that Gus had wanted her to come back. Why else would he have insisted she be given the small compass along with the terms of his will? She'd told Gus that she was pregnant, having a baby alone. He might have been trying to show her a way home, to remind her where her family roots lay.

Muirinn scrubbed her hands over her face quickly as she heard tires crunching up the driveway, telling herself it would be okay; she wasn't trapped here anymore. She could go back to New York anytime before the twelve months were up if things weren't working out. She could hire a publisher at any point she chose. *She* was the one in control here.

Smoothing errant tendrils of hair back from her face, Muirinn adjusted her sweater and went to meet the police.

"Could have been kids," Officer Ted Gage said as he stared at the papers scattered under the desk, thumbs hooked into his gun belt. "Incidents of vandalism often flare up during the summer holidays." His gaze tracked round the room. "Kids probably thought Gus's place was still empty."

"So you're not sending crime scene techs or anything?" Muirinn asked from the doorway.

He shrugged. "That's for the movies. We only dust for prints in major crimes. And nothing was stolen—"

"Not that I *know* of," she interrupted.

"That footprint is pretty big for a kid, Gage," said Jett. "I'd say about a size 12."

"I can point you to several kids with feet that size," he said around the gum between his teeth.

"Well, why don't you see if you can match one of them up to this print?"

"That's a lot of lab time and resources for a possible mischief or vandalism charge." He glanced sideways at Muirinn, a whisper of hostility beneath his deceptive easy-breezy style. Unease fingered into Muirinn.

"Look," he said suddenly. "I'll send someone around later. Depending on our caseload."

Muirinn was beyond exhausted now. She just wanted to go to bed. She thanked the cop, saw him out.

Jett hung back. "Would you like me to stay, Muirinn?"

She knew how difficult it must be for him to make the offer, and all she truly wanted to answer was *yes*.

"I'll be fine, thank you. Officer Gage is right, it's probably just vandalism with the place being empty and all. I can call 9-1-1 if the kids come back. Somehow I doubt that they will."

Jett didn't look so sure.

She wondered if his hesitancy was because of Officer Gage's chilly attitude toward her. Or because it seemed pretty darn clear that someone *had* been after something in her grandfather's office. For all Muirinn knew, they'd found what they'd been looking for, and had taken it. And she had no way of knowing what it was.

He reached for a pad of paper by the phone, scribbled something down, then ripped off the top sheet. "Here's my number." He looked directly into her eyes. "If you need help, Muirinn, I can be over right away. I live next door."

"Next door?"

"I've taken over my parents' house."

She felt the blood drain from her face.

His gaze skimmed over her tummy again, and she wanted to explain, to tell him that she was single; that she'd do anything for a second chance.

But he was married. He had a family.

And damn if they didn't all live right next door. Muirinn felt vaguely nauseous at the idea of facing the other woman. She told herself that she was tough, she could handle it. She'd been through enough in her life to know that.

So instead of justifying herself, she became defensive. "You're just dying to judge me, aren't you, Jett?"

"I gave up judging you a long time ago, Muirinn. What you do is none of my business."

And neither was his business hers. Yet here he stood, in her life again. And his words rang hollow.

"Look, I'm tired, Jett. I don't want to argue. I need to get some sleep."

He studied her for a long moment. "You always did get the last word in."

"No, Jett. You got the last word eleven years ago when you told me you hated me, and that I should never, ever come back."

His mouth flattened. "Muirinn—"

She swung the door open. "Go, please."

And he stepped out into the storm-whipped darkness.

She slammed the door shut behind him, flipping the lock with a sharp click. Then she slumped against the wood, allowing the hot tears to come as she listened to the tires of his truck crunching down the driveway.

Jett stood at the floor-to-ceiling windows in his living room, rain writhing over the panes as he watched the yellow glow coming from the kitchen window of Gus's house on the neighboring knoll.

He spun around, pacing the floor. What was he supposed to do?

Tell her?

After all these years?

No. He couldn't. He'd done what he had for a reason—and Gus had helped him do it.

He cursed viciously.

Seeing her pregnant now, back here in Safe Harbor…the irony just made everything more complicated.

Jett poured himself a whiskey in spite of the hour and took a long, hard swig, felt the burn in his chest. He exhaled slowly. He had no choice but to ride out this storm that was Muirinn O'Donnell. If she stayed true to form, she'd probably be gone within twelve months.

He wondered again about the father of her baby; where he was, whether they were married. There was a chance that Muirinn's husband would suddenly show up next door and join her. How in hell was he going to swallow *that?*

At least Troy was away at summer camp for a few weeks, because he was the one person who stood to lose the most in this situation. And Jett did not want his boy to get hurt.

He could not allow Muirinn to do that Troy.

There was just no way he was going to tell his son that Muirinn O'Donnell was his mother—that ten years ago she'd simply given him away in a private adoption.

He wasn't going to tell Muirinn, either, that he'd named their son after her father out of some deep need to connect his boy to his mother's side of the family.

In retrospect, Jett recognized that he'd probably been trying to tie himself back to Muirinn in some subconscious way, hoping she'd come back.

And now she *was* back.

Living right next door. Another baby on the way. Another man somewhere in her life. And before too long, she'd surely be gone again.

Right or wrong, the only way Jett could ever tell Muirinn the truth was if she somehow proved herself to him. She needed to show that she was worthy of her own son; that she'd stay, and not hurt Troy.

As she'd once hurt him.

Chapter 3

Muirinn awakened to a warm and sunny morning, but inside her gut a tiny icicle of unease was growing. As she poured her morning cup of decaf, she glanced at Gus's laptop and the envelope of photos that she'd put on the long dining room table.

Could that laptop and those photographs be what the burglars were searching for last night? She'd removed them from the attic and taken them down to her bedroom mere hours before the break-in. Had her grandfather really been poking into the old Tolkin mystery again? Was that why he was at the mine when he died?

Nothing made sense to her.

Muirinn blew out a heavy breath of air and looked out the window at the clear cobalt sky—blue as Jett's eyes. Her gaze shifted slowly over to his deck, jutting out over the trees next door.

An American flag snapped in the breeze, colorful against

the distant white peaks. Jett had found Gus's body—he could tell her more. But Muirinn didn't want to talk to him.

Not after last night.

She needed to stay away from him.

Her best option was to talk directly to the Safe Harbor police. She'd go to the station later today, right after she met with Rick Frankl, the editor of Safe Harbor Publishing. She'd already left a message at Rick's office for him to call her to set up an appointment. But first she wanted to look inside Gus's laptop.

Muirinn set her mug down, seated herself at Gus's rustic wood table and powered up the computer. Immediately, a message box flashed up onto the screen asking for a password.

She tried several possibilities, including O'Donnell family names, and the name of the cat.

Nothing worked.

The only way she was going to access this laptop was with the aid of a computer tech who could circumvent the password protection. She also needed a tech to help reconnect the hard drive up in the attic office. Perhaps Rick Frankl could recommend one.

Muirinn reached instead for the brown envelope and slid the black-and-white crime scene photos out. She spread them over the table. Most of the images she recognized from the book her grandfather had written years ago on the Tolkin massacre. But there were a few other images she didn't think she'd seen before. She picked one up—a shot of bootprints in shiny black mud, a ruler positioned alongside the impressions.

Muirinn flipped it over, read the notation on the back. *Missing Photo #3. Bomber tracks.*

She frowned. Quickly, she flipped over the rest of the photographs she didn't recognize, laying them all facedown on

the table. On the back of each one was a similar set of nota-
tions, all with the word *Missing* scrawled in her grandfather's
bold hand.

What did this mean?

Surely her grandfather had given up trying to actually *solve*
the Tolkin murders? Unless…she stared at the images strewn
all over the table. Unless there was *new* evidence.

No. It wasn't possible.

Was it?

She turned the images faceup again, selected a photo of a
mining headframe—a rusted A-shaped metal skeleton that
loomed over a small boarded-up shack. She flipped it over,
read the back: *Missing photo #8. Sodwana headframe.
Bomber used as entry to mine?*

She'd never heard any theory about the bomber using the
Sodwana headframe to gain access to the mine. As far as she
could recall, the old Sodwana shaft was literally miles from
the actual underground blast location near D-shaft. FBI investigators had always surmised that the bomber had been
someone working inside the mine that day, someone who'd
crossed the picket line with her father.

Muirinn realized that she didn't even know *which* shaft Gus
had been found in. Had it been Sodwana?

She shot another look at Jett's deck, inhaling deeply. He
would know…but before she could articulate another thought,
the phone rang.

Muirinn jumped at the sudden shrill noise, then, clearing
her throat, she lifted the receiver. "Hello?"

"Muirinn? This is Rick Frankl, returning your call. Welcome
to Safe Harbor—I'd love to meet with you sometime today."

Smoothing her hand over her hair, Muirinn glanced up at
the wall clock. She was nervous about meeting Rick and

taking over a small business she knew little about. "How are you fixed for time this afternoon, Rick?"

"Around noon would be perfect."

"I'll be there."

"Looking forward to it—we all are. And I can't begin to tell you how sorry we are for your loss, Muirinn. Gus was our cornerstone here. We *all* miss him."

She swallowed against the lump forming in her throat. "Thank you, Rick."

"His office is ready and waiting for you. We've left everything as it was, apart from some cleaning after the break-in—"

"Break-in?" Her hand tightened on the receiver. "When?"

"Two nights ago. Someone managed to disable the alarm system and come in via his office window."

"Was anything stolen?"

"Nothing that we can ascertain. Gus's desk drawers were ransacked and his computer was turned on, but that was it. We did file a report with the police, of course. Apparently there's not much more they can do in a case like this. The cop who responded said it was probably just vandals."

Muirinn shot another glance at the laptop, the photos spread out over the table. "Which cop?"

"Officer Ted Gage."

After finalizing the details of the meeting, Muirinn slowly replaced the handset, a coolness cloaking her skin. *Both* Gus's offices ransacked? This was more than coincidence.

And why hadn't Officer Gage mentioned this to her last night?

Muirinn quickly gathered up the photos and slid them back into the envelope. To be safe, she unlocked a drawer hidden in the side of Gus's thick, handcrafted table.

She placed both the envelope and the laptop into it, but as

she was about to shut and lock the drawer, she caught sight of a small bottle of pills in the drawer.

She picked up container and read the label. *Digoxin.*

Gus's heart medication.

Closing her fist around the bottle, holding it tight against her chest, Muirinn walked back to the window, eyes hot with emotion. Her grandfather had never mentioned his heart condition to her. But while that hurt, it wasn't surprising. Gus had routinely refused to acknowledge his encroaching age or ill health, and he used to drink all sorts of herb teas to ward off the inevitable.

Comfrey had been his favorite—knitbone tea, he'd called it. *"To knit them old bones."*

Her chest tightened at the memory of his words, and she swiped away an errant tear.

Gus had always said crying was a useless waste of time. If something worried you, you went out and fixed it. And that was exactly what she had to do now. She needed to get to the bottom of these break-ins. And she needed to know why Gus had been looking into the Tolkin Mine murders again.

Collecting herself, she locked the drawer, slipped the key and the pills into her purse, and glanced into the hall mirror. Tucking a strand of hair behind her ear, she scooped up the keys to Gus's Dodge truck.

She'd go into town, meet with Rick at the paper, and then head over to the police department.

Because now she really wanted some answers.

The truck wouldn't start.

Muirinn turned the ignition again, and it just clicked. The oil light on the dash glowed red.

Damn.

Muirinn climbed out of the cab, hoisted up her skirt and got onto hands and knees to look underneath the vehicle. Sure enough, there in the gravel was a big, dark pool of glistening liquid.

Stretching to reach under the truck, she tapped her finger lightly into the puddle so she could smell what it was.

"Muirinn!"

She jumped, banging her head on the undercarriage. Cursing, she backed out from under the vehicle and sat up, heart thumping.

"Is that *you*, Muirinn?"

She blinked up into bright sunlight at the silhouetted form of an old woman bent double, peering down at her with a bunch of purple flowers clutched in her hand.

"Mrs. Wilkie?" she said, rubbing her head. "My God, you half startled me to death!"

"Are you all right, dear? Did you hurt yourself?" she said in a warm, gravelly voice that Muirinn remembered so well from her youth.

"I'm fine." She got to her feet awkwardly, dusting her knees off. "I was just checking out the oil leak." The back of her head throbbed where she'd banged it, and her baby was kicking. Muirinn placed her hand on her belly, calming her baby and herself.

"I heard you'd come back, sprite." Mrs. Wilkie angled her head as she spoke, wrinkles fanning out from her intelligent gray eyes. Quicksilver, who'd materialized from nowhere at the sound of Mrs. Wilkie's voice, was purring and rubbing against the old lady's legs.

"I was just coming up to feed the cat, and to put some fresh flowers inside your house. I've also got some new herbs for tea. Sorry I scared you, dear."

Muirinn noted that Mrs. Wilkie's body had bowed even further to age, like a gnarled tree that had spent its life on a windswept shore. But she was still beautiful, her face tanned and creased in a way that spoke of kindness, her eyes still bright and quick. A thick gray braid hung over her shoulder, and she wore a long gypsy skirt, riotous with color. Muirinn wondered just how old the woman was now. To her mind, Mrs. Wilkie had seemed old forever, like a mythical crone.

She gave the hardy old dear a shaky smile, adrenaline still coursing through her body. "Thank you. It's good to see you, Mrs. Wilkie. I heard from the lawyer that you'd been taking excellent care of Gus, and I see you've been feeding Quicksilver, but I—"

Muirinn was about to say she no longer needed daily housekeeping services. Guilt stopped her. This woman had been here for Gus—she'd been a companion to him. Which was more than Muirinn could say for herself.

Mrs. Wilkie had lived in a small cottage down by the bay on Gus's property as long as Muirinn could remember. Even though it was now Muirinn's land, there was probably an official lease that still needed to be honored. Plus, the woman likely relied on the minimal income Gus had paid her, whatever it was.

Muirinn needed to go easy, go slow. Give things time.

"You were saying, dear?" Mrs. Wilkie was watching her intently, waiting.

"It's...nothing."

"Well, it's a terrible thing about Gus. I miss him. But it's good to see *you* back, Muirinn, and to see that you are expecting, too," Mrs. Wilkie said softly. "Are you going to have the baby here in Safe Harbor?"

Muirinn realized that she hadn't really thought that far ahead. "I... yes, I am."

"Well, if you go running into any trouble, you know where to find me. I've helped deliver my fair share of children, including my two nephews."

"I know. Thank you, Mrs. Wilkie." Muirinn was aware that Lydia Wilkie had once been a nurse who'd moved gradually into midwifery and naturopathy. She'd always had a keen interest in herbs and the natural healing practices of aboriginal peoples. When they were kids, Muirinn and Jett used to peer into her cottage window down by the water, pretending they were spying on the Good Witch because she was always boiling some herbal concoction on her blackened wood stove.

"Now, you call me Lydia," she said.

Muirinn smiled. "I can't. You've been *Mrs. Wilkie* to me forever."

Mrs. Wilkie's face crumpled into a grin. She took Muirinn's hand firmly in her gnarled one. "It's so good to have you home, sprite. Gus would be mighty pleased. Especially to have a small one around the house again."

Muirinn nodded, emotion prickling into her eyes again at the sound of her old nickname. Damn these pregnancy hormones and this trip down memory lane. "I know he would," she answered quietly.

I just wish I'd come home sooner.

Mrs. Wilkie turned, her gypsy skirt swirling around in a rainbow of color as she scuttled up the steps toward the front door. She unlocked it with her own key.

"Do you know any decent mechanics in town?" Muirinn called after her, vaguely uneasy with the idea of this woman coming and going into her house at will.

"Why, Jett next door could fix that truck for you, Muirinn. I'll just go right on inside, put these flowers down on the table and call him." She disappeared through the front door.

"Mrs. Wilkie! *Wait*—"

The old woman peeked back out the door. "What is it, love?"

"I…I'd rather call a mechanic from town."

"What nonsense. You've been away too long, sprite." She smiled. "We look after each other out here." And with that she vanished into the house.

Muirinn sank onto the bottom stair, tears threatening to overwhelm her again. She dropped her face into her hands fighting to hold it all in.

Pregnancy was making her so darn emotional about coming home.

So had seeing Jett.

Her feelings for him were still powerful—feelings for a man she could never have again.

A man she'd never stopped loving.

Jett found her sitting on stairs, crying.

His heart torqued and his throat tightened—the old Muirinn had never cried.

He shut of his ignition and got out of his truck. As he approached her, he felt his mouth go dry. She was wearing a chiffon skirt in pale spring colors. She had dirt on her smooth legs and he could see way too much of her thigh for male comfort. Her fiery hair hung wild and loose around her slender shoulders, glinting with gold strands in the sun.

"Hey," he said softly, sitting awkwardly beside her, trying to restrain himself from putting his arm around her and comforting her. "What's up?"

She sniffed, then laughed dryly as she smeared tears and dirt across her face. "God, I'm a stupid wreck. It's…it's the hormones." She nodded toward the truck. "Gus's truck didn't start. It was just a last little straw…" her voice faltered, hitched and flooded again with emotion. "I...miss him, Jett." Tears came again. *"I really miss him."*

And then he did touch her. He put his arm around her shoulders, drew her close and held her while she left her grief out. And he knew it was a mistake.

The warm curve of her breast, the firm swell of her belly against his torso, the exhilarating sensation of her thigh against his jeans...they did things to his body. Clouded his mind. With them came a raw and powerful protectiveness that surged through his chest, and Jett felt afraid—of what this could mean to all of them.

He was crossing a line. One look at her and he was falling in love all over again, when all he wanted was a reason to push her away, a reason to hate her, to despise her for what she'd done in the past.

But in this moment, the lines between past and present were blurring.

"I just wish I could have been here for Gus, then maybe... maybe this wouldn't have happened."

"What do you mean? His death?" Jett's voice came out thick.

She glanced up, luminous eyes red-rimmed from crying, and his heart squeezed all over again.

"You led the search-and-rescue team that found Gus, Jett. Tell me about it. Where exactly did you find his body?"

"Muirinn—"

"Please, Jett, everything. Step by step. I need to know."

He moistened his lips and nodded.

"When we first got the report that Gus was missing, we really had nothing to go on. Then on the thirteenth day, we got a break. A hunter called the police tip line to say he'd been on his way out into the bush almost two weeks earlier, when he'd seen Gus walking inside the perimeter fence of Tolkin Mine.

He hadn't thought anything of it until he'd returned and heard the news. We brought dogs in immediately, set them to work on the Tollkin property. They led us straight to the shaft—"

"Sodwana shaft?"

He frowned. "Yes, why?"

She hesitated. "Just wondering."

"The grate covering the man-way inside the headframe building had been pulled off. So we went down with ropes, flashlights." He paused, watching her, compassion filling his heart. "We found him down there. On the 300 level."

Muirinn's neck tensed. She swallowed. "What's on the 300 level?"

"More tunnels. Another man-way that leads further down, possibly as far as the 800 level."

"Who was the hunter who called in that tip, Jett?"

"The cops don't know. It's an anonymous tip line."

Her cheeks flushed with frustration, or maybe anger— he'd always found that so sexy, the way her complexion betrayed her emotions so easily.

"So, basically, my grandfather might've been saved if he'd just taken the trouble to tell someone where he was going that day. Why didn't he?"

"Who knows, Muirinn. You knew he was stubborn."

"But didn't you guys think it was odd that he was down there, down that shaft?"

"I had questions, sure," said Jett. "But the ME and the police went through everything. So did Dr. Callaghan. Pat had been treating Gus's heart condition for some time already. There was no evidence of foul play of any sort, if that's what you're thinking."

She bit her lip to stop it from wobbling, looked away.

"Hey—" he cupped her jaw, turned her face back to his,

and immediately regretted the impulse. "Gus was a really eccentric old guy, Muirinn, even more so these past few years. This was in keeping with his character."

Tears pooled in her eyes again, and Jett couldn't stop himself from asking. "You'd have known all this about Gus if you'd come to see him," he said quietly. "Why, Muirinn? Why didn't you ever come home to see your grandfather?"

She held his eyes, silent for several beats, something unreadable darkening her features. Then she sighed heavily. "I sent Gus plane tickets, Jett, so he could come to see me in New York."

"Yeah, he wasn't that impressed with the city. He told us about it."

Her lips flattened. "And for his birthday, I sent him a ticket to Spain. I met him in Madrid. Gus had a thing for Hemingway— he wanted to see a bullfight..." Tears spilled down her cheeks again. "Damn, I'm so sorry," she said brushing them away.

"Sorry for what? *Caring?*"

Her eyes shot up to his.

"Look, I guess I just don't understand why you didn't even come back for his memorial service, Muirinn. Or when you first heard he was missing."

"I didn't *know* he was missing!"

"*Someone* must have told you."

"I was unreachable, Jett, on assignment in the remote jungles of West Papua—"

"With no cell phone? No satellite connection, nothing?"

"Nothing." She rubbed her face. "That was the whole point of the assignment, to be inaccessible. For myself, an anthropologist and a photographer to spend some time with one of the world's last truly isolated tribes. Part of my story was to be about that sense of isolation. Our goal was to feel it."

"But you were—*are*—pregnant."

"And in good health. Women in those tribes have been bearing children in that jungle for centuries. The photographer was also a paramedic. I was not at risk."

"What if there had been an emergency?"

"That's the point, Jett. Our society can't conceive of living without phones, Internet, radios. We don't know how to cope on our own anymore. We go into a total panic at the mere *notion* of not being in contact, but it's not necessary. Besides, I grew up here, remember? My grandfather raised me to be self-sufficient."

"Stubborn is more like it," he muttered.

She glanced at him. "You disapprove of me."

Jett inhaled deeply, thinking how she'd run off pregnant with *his* baby, never allowing him to share in the joy of a pregnancy, the birth of his son.

"It's not just you that you need to think about," he said. "You have a responsibility toward a child now."

"You're still angry at me, aren't you?" she whispered.

He *wanted* to be. He needed *something* to shield himself from this woman. Anger was all he had to protect himself right now.

Jett got up suddenly, went to the truck.

"You're avoiding my question," she called after him.

"I'm doing what Mrs. Wilkie called me over to do," he said coolly, as he opened the door. "What happened when you tried to start it?"

"Nothing at all. I think it's an oil leak," Muirinn said, getting up and following him to the truck, sun burning down hot on her head as it rose higher in the clear blue sky.

He climbed into the cab. "There's a bunch of gray silt on the floor here," he said, turning the key in the ignition. It clicked but the engine didn't start. "You'll need to clean this thing out if you want your city clothes to stay all fancy," he said, shooting her a glance. "And you're going to need better sandals, too, if you actually want to get around."

"I was going into the office, to meet Rick Frankl," she replied crisply. "And then I was going to see the police chief—"

He crooked up a brow. "Chief Moran?"

"Whoever."

He turned the key again and frowned. "Oil light is on."

"Doesn't take a genius to see that."

Jett scowled, popped the hood and climbed out of the cab.

"What do you want to see Moran for? To complain about Gage?" He checked the oil as he spoke, then stripped off his shirt.

Muirinn's heart skipped a beat as her gaze tracked over his naked torso, down to the dark hair that ran in a whorl into his jeans. Heat flooded her veins and she swallowed, feeling a small bead of sweat roll down between her breasts.

His eyes darkened—he was clearly aware of the effect his naked, sun-browned abs were having on her. This made her cheeks flush red and her pulse race. "I…uh, there was another break-in, at Gus's newspaper office."

"What?"

"According to Rick, nothing was taken," she said, her voice husky. She cleared her throat. "Officer Gage responded to that incident as well. He should've said something to me, and I intend to take this up with his superior, because this can't be a coincidence. *Someone* is looking for *something* that belonged to Gus."

He was looking at her mouth. But he tore his gaze away, got down on his haunches and slid himself under the truck.

Muirinn stared at him, the way his thigh muscles flexed under the fabric of his jeans. Her mouth turned dry. This was wrong, so wrong.

"Looks like the oil sump was ruptured by something—a

sharp rock maybe," he called out from under the vehicle. "It's been leaking out for some time."

He came out from under the truck and got to his feet in a fluid, powerful movement. He reached into the cab for a rag. "A new sump, some oil and it'll be good as new," he said wiping his hands on the rag, avoiding her eyes now. He put his shirt back on, ruffled his hand through his hair and then hesitated, as if unsure, nervous.

Then he handed Muirinn her purse from inside the truck. "I'll drive you into town. I can pick up a new sump and oil while you meet with Frankl, then I'll go with you to the cops."

Anxiety licked at her. "You don't have to do this, Jett."

He moistened his lips, still avoiding her eyes. "Yeah, I do. I don't like these break-ins, either. And I don't like the way Ted Gage treated you. Besides, Chief Don Moran can be a bear at the best of times—"

"Don—is *he* chief now? As in Bill's little brother?"

"Keeping it in the family, those Morans." He smiled, but it didn't quite reach into his eyes. "Things really went to the collective Moran head when the youngest brother's wife was elected mayor. Now they think they run this town."

Jett touched her elbow gently as he led her to his truck.

"You mean Chalky Moran's wife? Who did he marry?"

He opened the passenger door for her. "Kate Lonsdale. She's been mayor for the past year now."

They drove in tense silence along the twisting dirt road that clung to the ragged shoreline, dust billowing out behind them.

Muirinn wished she could rewind the last half hour, retract Mrs. Wilkie's call to Jett. She should never have let this happen, never should have let him touch her. Because she'd seen in his eyes that, hidden behind that brittle shell, he still felt something for her. And she sure as hell felt *everything* for him.

But he was married. Out of bounds.

And Muirinn owed it to his wife, his son, to *him,* to stay away, leave the past where it belonged.

She felt him glance at her and she swallowed, cheeks flushing hot as she looked away.

And in that moment she knew it was too late. She was already in trouble.

They both were.

Chapter 4

Chief Don Moran shut his office door and motioned for Muirinn and Jett to take a seat. Through his glass walls Muirinn could see Ted Gage watching them intently from his desk across the bullpen. She could feel the other officers watching, too, and wished Moran would lower the blinds.

"What can I do for you, Ms. O'Donnell?" Moran said as he took his seat on the opposite side of his metal desk, his eyes flicking to Jett. He was clearly not surprised to see her back in town, nor was he overly thrilled about it.

Don looked unnervingly like his much older brother, William "Bill" Moran, from his father's first marriage. It was as if Don had somehow morphed into his brother with age.

While Don had been just a twenty-two-year-old rookie at the time of the Tolkin blast, Bill had been the Safe Harbor police chief. It was Bill who'd approached Muirinn's mother in the snow that day, and told her that her husband was among the dead.

Seeing Don looking so much like his brother threw Muirinn off guard. Gray images of that tragic, snowy spring morning suddenly filled her mind, and for a disconcerting moment, she was nine years old again.

She cleared her throat. "My grandfather's—*my*—house at Mermaid's Cove was broken into last night—"

"I saw the report, yes. Vandals, most likely."

She leaned forward. "I don't think so, Chief Moran. I've just learned that Gus's newspaper office was also broken into, two days ago. Nothing was taken there, either."

Moran glanced discreetly at his watch, telegraphing mild impatience. "What is it that seems to be the problem, Ms. O'Donnell?"

"I believe the break-ins have to be connected, and that someone was looking for something in Gus's papers or computer files."

His eyes turned flat, inscrutable. Silence hung for a beat. "What gives you that idea?"

Muirinn felt Jett stiffen beside her. She placed her hand on his knee to steady him—and take support from his proximity. "Pardon me, Chief, but what *wouldn't* give me that idea? Gus was—" suddenly she didn't want to mention the Tolkin file, the photographs, what Gus might have been working on. She had a bad feeling about it all, about the way the other cops were eyeing her from the bullpen.

He waited for her to continue.

"I…was just hoping that you'd have one of your men look into it."

He inhaled deeply, and stood. "We treat all our cases with due consideration, Ms. O'Donnell." His gaze lingered on Jett for a moment, his jaw tight. "And we allocate our resources accordingly. But we're extremely short-staffed, given the city budget cuts."

"Looks like you have a few men to spare at the moment." Jett interjected, nodding his head to the guys watching from the bullpen.

Moran's eye twitched slightly. "I'll see what we can do." He went to the door and swung it open, waiting for them to leave, his features expressionless.

"Thank you," Muirinn said, getting to her feet, but she hesitated in the doorway, bolstered by Jett at her side. "Chief Moran, why did it take so long to find him? I mean, my grandfather was missing for over two weeks. Didn't *anyone* see his truck parked out at the Tolkin site?"

"There was no vehicle parked out there, Ms. O'Donnell."

"What?" She shot a questioning glance at Jett. "No one told me that."

"Our assumption is that Gus hiked out to the mine."

"You're kidding. With a heart condition? That's fifteen to twenty miles out of town. In summer heat. I—"

"Ms. O'Donnell, I really am very sorry for your loss, but I can't speak to your grandfather's health condition, nor to his state of mind at the time of his disappearance. All I can tell you is that the ME determined the cause of death to be a heart attack." His voice softened slightly. "If you want to know more, why don't you go talk to Doc Callaghan? She was treating your grandfather."

"I will. I just don't understand why it took everyone so long to find him down there," she said quietly. Now that she'd actually voiced it, she was convinced that there was something seriously amiss with the circumstances surrounding her grandfather's death.

"Really, there's nothing more to it than meets the eye, Ms. O'Donnell." Moran smiled.

She met his gaze. "Yes," she said. "I'm sure it's all…coincidence."

Jett thanked the chief for his time, then placed his hand gently on her elbow as he guided Muirinn out of the police station into the harsh sunlight. She put on her shades.

"You're shaking," he said softly.

"I—" she exhaled nervously. "I guess I am. Must be low blood sugar or something. Why didn't you tell me that Gus didn't drive out to the mine?"

"I thought you knew those details." Concern softened his blue eyes. "Have you eaten, Muirinn?"

"I…I just haven't been hungry."

"Come, we're getting some lunch into you."

"Jett, I should really just go home."

"Food first, then I'll take you home." His tone brooked no argument, and Muirinn allowed him to escort her down to a small café patio with red umbrellas near the harbor, feeling that each second longer she spent with him, the further she was headed past the point of no return.

People stared openly as they walked, and her sense of unease deepened. The rumors had no doubt rippled through town—Safe Harbor's prodigal daughter had returned. And now she was seven months' pregnant, being escorted around town by a married man.

She wondered, too, how they must judge her for missing Gus's funeral, coming after the fact to claim her inheritance.

They had no idea what remorse she was feeling at not having returned once in eleven years to see her grandfather. Even though she'd met with Gus on neutral territory over the years, she now realized that it had probably hurt Gus beyond words that she hadn't come home.

The irony wasn't lost on her.

She'd done it solely to avoid Jett, yet here he was, the man who had her back now. And she realized just how deeply she'd missed him.

And how much trouble she was getting herself into.

"Jett," she said softly as he pulled out a chair for her at a table under a red umbrella, feeling people watching. "I really don't think this is a good idea."

"Sit, Muirinn. Just eat something, and then I'll take you right home."

That was the kind of man he was. Like his father, Jett was hardwired to save, rescue. Protect. Emotion choked her inexplicably. She took a seat and a second to compose herself.

He avoided her gaze as he reached for the menu, but the small muscle at the base of his jaw pulsed. He was as conflicted as she was, and Muirinn could see it.

I'm sorry to have put you in this position. I promise to stay out of your way after today, Jett.

Jett stared blindly at the menu, unable to focus on the items. What in hell was he really looking for here, right this minute? With her?

For a brief shining nanosecond, he knew. This wasn't about trying to help her figure out what had gone down with Gus, or about helping her with the truck. *He wanted her back.*

He wanted her to prove herself to him, so he could feel safe enough to tell her about their son. So he could tell her that he wasn't married.

Mostly, he needed her to come clean about having given his baby away behind his back. He wanted to hear her say that she was sorry. He wanted to know that she'd felt remorse.

And he wanted to be sure that she was going to stay.

Only then could he tell her about Troy.

Only then could he trust himself to be near her, because his body sure as hell had different ideas from his mind.

Jett blew out a breath, and dragged his fingers through his hair. "What're you having?"

"Orange juice."

He glanced up. "You need more. You're eating for two."

"I'm not really hungry."

He flipped the menu shut, ordered a sandwich, juice and coffee. "Now tell me what's going on, Muirinn," he said as the waitress left.

"You mean with the break-ins?"

No, with you, the baby, the father, that fancy magazine job—everything.

"Yeah, with the break-ins," he said instead. "You're clearly suspicious about Gùs's death, and you asked me earlier specifically if he'd been found down the Sodwana shaft. And I want to know why."

She fiddled with her napkin, her clear green eyes holding his for a moment, and a band squeezed tight across his chest. She was so strikingly gorgeous, and—though he hated to admit it—even more attractive to him now than she'd been a decade ago.

There was a new sophistication, a wisdom in her eyes, yet it was balanced by a softness that came with pregnancy, and with the pain of the loss she'd just experienced.

She'd been all wild, rough edges when she was nineteen; a flat-out challenge. He suspected that he hadn't been much different himself. Hell, they were just kids; their relationship as combative as it had been loving. It had been about the sparring, the fun. The sex.

Until it had all gone bad.

"I think Gus was investigating the old Tolkin murders—"

"Muirinn—" he interjected, leaning forward. "—Gus was *always* thinking about the Tolkin murders. That's nothing new."

"I think he might have come across some new crime scene photos, Jett." She lowered her voice, glancing at the tables around theirs. "I believe those photos and Gus's laptop could have been the target of the break-ins, because I'd removed them from his attic desk just before going to sleep that night."

Jett frowned. "What's in the laptop?"

"I don't know yet—it's password-protected. But Rick Frankl is sending a tech around later."

Unease trickled into Jett, along with worry.

Damn.

The last thing he wanted right now was to worry about Muirinn. What he wanted was space, to think. Her proximity was clouding his mind, driving his libido to distraction. He inhaled deeply. "Will you let me know what you find?"

"Sure," she said, reaching for her shades.

He placed his hand over hers, stopping her. "Muirinn? You *will* call?"

She cast her eyes down. "I don't want to have to call you, Jett," she whispered.

"Why?"

She swallowed, looked up slowly, her eyes glittering with emotion. "You're attached, Jett. You have a family. A wife."

For a very long beat he said nothing, and a heated current thrummed between them.

Don't say anything stupid here, buddy. Think of Troy.

"Where were your wife and Troy going yesterday?" she asked suddenly.

He hesitated, then lied by omission. "She was taking him

to summer camp," he said, circumnavigating the part about his divorce five years ago, knowing at the same time he'd just started digging a hole that he was going to have one hell of a time climbing out of.

"What's your wife's name, Jett?"

"Kim." At least that wasn't a lie, exactly.

Her jaw quivered and she bit her lip.

Guilt stabbed through him. He told himself he was entitled to do this, she probably had a man waiting for her somewhere, perhaps even coming to join her. And suddenly he couldn't stop himself from asking.

"What about the father of your baby, Muirinn? Where is he?"

She turned and stared out over the sea. "I'm flying solo, Jett," she said very quietly. "I'm doing this on my own."

Something hot ripped through him. "What do you mean?"

She sighed. "Things just never worked out. I...I could never seem to find the right guy."

So she'd done it again.

She'd gotten pregnant with her lover's child, and then she'd abandoned the man, not giving him a chance, *a choice,* to be a father. It instantly tempered his feelings toward her.

Jett could remember *exactly* what it had felt like. He recalled just how badly she could dig the knife into his heart, and twist.

How she might do it again—if he let her.

He cleared his throat. "And what exactly were you looking for in a guy, Muirinn?" he said coolly.

She breathed out nervously. "You, I think."

He felt the blood rush from his head.

"God," she whispered, panic flaring in her eyes. "That... that was a terrible mistake." She got up so fast she knocked her chair back onto the patio. "I…I am so sorry, Jett." She spun around, walking as fast she could.

Jett stared, glued to his seat for a nanosecond before his brain kicked back into gear. Then he leaped up, digging into his back pocket for his wallet. He dumped a wad of cash onto the table, and ran after her into the street. "Muirinn! Stop!"

She didn't look back.

Instead, she waved wildly to a passing cab.

She was in the door, and the cab was pulling off, before he reached her.

Jett watched the brake lights flare at the stop sign at the end of the block. Then the cab turned the corner and vanished.

He stood there in the street, shell-shocked.

She still loved him.

She'd never stopped.

Exhilaration mounted inside him like a wild thing, coupled tightly with fear for his child. Because she was still capable of dumping him—just as she'd obviously dumped the father of her new baby.

"If O'Donnell has accessed that laptop, it means she's seen the old man's theory," said the voice on the phone. "It's only a matter of time before she connects the rest of the dots."

"Christ, if this gets out—"

"It *can't*."

"So what do we do now?"

Silence. Heavy, loaded silence.

"Oh, sweet Jesus, no. If something happens to Muirinn O'Donnell it's going send red flags up all over the goddamn place!"

"Then we control those flags, because—" The voice lowered. "—the alternative is far, far worse."

"What about *him?*"

"We don't know how deep he is in yet, which is why this must happen fast—understand? One step at a time."

More silence.

"Look, we can handle this—we've managed worse before, remember?" The voice went even quieter still. "Find a way. Just make sure it looks like an accident."

The phone clicked.

Chapter 5

Muirinn powered up Gus's laptap.

After fleeing Jett in the cab yesterday she'd spent the afternoon tidying her grandfather's attic office, and the evening going through the newspaper company books. Her sleep that night had been fitful, and she'd awakened late in the morning to learn from Mrs. Wilkie that Jett had quietly come around at 5:00 a.m to replace the fuel sump in the truck.

Clearly, he'd been avoiding her.

It was for the best.

Muirinn exhaled in exasperation as she pulled her hair back into a severe ponytail. She was utterly mortified by what had come out of her mouth yesterday. Even more disturbing was the spark of need she'd glimpsed in his eyes, the tenderness she'd felt in his touch.

It was all still there—their old bond, the raw, simmering attraction. She and Jett were like flame to fireworks. Always had been. There was just no way she could be in his presence, or he in hers, without things exploding.

She'd send him a thank-you note for fixing the truck, because her promise to herself—her *vow* to him—was to stay the hell out of his life until things settled down, and his wife and child returned.

She rubbed her face angrily, and clicked open the file labeled *Tolkin.*

And with slow, mounting horror, she began to read what her grandfather had written.

According to Gus, the crime scene photographs labeled *missing* in the brown envelope, had "disappeared" from the Safe Harbor Police Department's evidence room twenty years ago, during the violent snowstorm that delayed the FBI post-blast team's arrival for forty-eight hours.

Since then they'd been in the possession of retired and recently deceased SHPD officer, Ike Potter.

Over the last few years, Ike, who'd been suffering from cancer, had become a close friend of Gus's. They'd played chess regularly at the Seven Seas Club. It was during these chess games that Ike had learned the sheer extent of Gus's obsession with the Tolkin murders and his desperate need for closure, to find out who had killed his son.

This knowledge had begun to wear Ike down, and on his deathbed, Ike had told Gus that he had wanted to come clean, to make peace with the past. And he'd told Gus his story, entrusting him with several crime scene photos that had been kept in a safe deposit box up until that point.

Muirinn scrolled further.

The night of the blizzard, Ike had returned to the police station to pick up a plug-in cable for his vehicle. That was when he'd witnessed a fellow SHPD officer in the dark, with a flashlight, removing the photos from police evidence. The officer had however been interrupted by someone else coming down the hall, and he'd hurriedly trashed them with department waste that was destined for routine incineration in a few hours.

Ike had waited until the coast was clear, then he'd retrieved the photographs and hidden them himself while he tried to figure out what was going on.

The photos were of bootprints taken outside and inside the Sodwana headframe building, and of prints inside the mine allegedly made by the bomber.

Muirinn's pulse accelerated.

It was Ike's belief that the prints documented in these photos had been compromised by someone in the SHPD before the FBI team could get in, contaminating the scene and thus sabotaging the investigation.

Muirinn scrolled faster through Gus's notes, tension squeezing her chest like a vise.

But Ike had died before finishing his whole story. And for some reason, he'd never blown the whistle until speaking to Gus.

There was also no mention of *which* SHPD officer had originally taken the photos from evidence. Muirinn had no means of knowing whether he—or she—was still even a cop. Twenty years was a long time.

Blown away by what she'd just read, Muirinn sat back to catch her breath. According to Gus's notes, more than one person in Safe Harbor had covered the tracks of the man who had killed her dad, and her mom by default. Nausea—and rage—began to swirl in her stomach.

She turned back to the computer. But the notes ended, the last questions posed: *Did bomber use Sodwana shaft to access D-shaft where bomb was planted? Did accomplice stand guard at headframe?*

Accomplice?

Perspiration prickled over Muirinn's skin.

This was even worse than she'd imagined. This was a conspiracy. The burglar must have been after this information.

And there was certainly no way she could trust the cops now.

Hurriedly, Muirinn emptied the photographs onto the table, spreading them out. She separated the photos labeled *missing* from the rest, and she picked up the image of bootprints made outside the Sodwana headframe building.

Were these the prints of an accomplice?

She selected another photo—of the prints in black mud allegedly made by the bomber himself. A chill crawled over her skin as she wondered whether the man who'd made them still walked the streets of Safe Harbor.

She got up and started pacing in front of the windows, her heart beating fast. She wondered just how far someone would go to keep this old secret buried.

Could they have killed Gus for this?

Who could she turn to? Not Jett. No way. She'd made a vow—she wasn't going to mess up his family.

She clasped her hand over the little bone compass at her neck. Whatever the answers, she owed it to Gus to find them, to see through what he'd started and secure the closure he'd sought so desperately for the last twenty years.

She owed her dad.

Her mom.

And Muirinn owed it to herself to finally put the past to rest. That Tolkin blast had torn her life apart. It was part of the reason she'd come to hate Safe Harbor, and had so desperately needed to leave it. And leaving had cost her so much.

Including her first child. And Jett.

Now she had a new baby on the way, a business to run. And she had a home she could really call her own—the childhood home that her father had crossed the picket line and died to keep, the home that Gus had stepped in to save from foreclosure after her parents' deaths. This just made her more determined to stay. Muirinn truly had something to fight for now, and she was not going to let whoever had destroyed her past destroy her future, too.

She moved closer to the window, staring absently at Jett's deck in the distance as her mind raced, and she was suddenly distracted by a sharp flash of light. Then another.

Muirinn went to a corner window where Gus's powerful telescope stood atop a tripod.

She swung the massive scope over to Jett's property, bent slightly and peered through the sight, adjusting the focus.

Surprise rippled through her.

Jett.

Standing on his deck, wearing only drawstring shorts slung low and baggy on taut hips. And he was aiming binoculars at her house…directly at the window in front of which she'd just been sitting.

Had he been watching her all this time?

But now she was watching him, and he was totally unaware. "Gotcha," she whispered.

She quickly sharpened the telescope's focus.

Her grandfather's equipment was state of the art—she could make out the individual ridges of muscle on Jett's sun-bronzed torso. He looked as though he'd just stepped out of a shower, hair damp and hanging over his brow.

From the privacy of her corner window, Muirinn couldn't help but study him, panning the telescope slowly over the length of his body, going lower and lower down his abs, following the whorl of dark hair into his shorts. Heat pooled low in her abdomen and she felt her nipples tingle.

Jett suddenly angled his binoculars over to her window.

Muirinn's breathing stalled.

Jett's body stiffened as he caught her looking at him from the side window. But he didn't lower his binoculars. He stared right back at her, a slow wry smile forming on his lips.

Stepping back quickly from the lens, she dragged her hands over her hair, face flushing hot. Panic started to circle.

Muirinn quickly reached forward and dropped the blinds. As if that could wipe out what had just happened.

She paced the dining room, swearing to herself. Truly, the best thing for both of them would be for her to get out of here, to leave Safe Harbor. Soon.

But she wasn't going to do that.

Gus had wanted her to come back.

And she had too much to fight for now. Damn, she had a *right* to be here, to make a life in Safe Harbor if she so chose.

She shot another glance at Gus's laptop, thinking again about the murders.

How had she manage to end up between a rock and a hard place like this, anyway? Frustration mounted in her, and it turned gradually to anger.

Jett had a responsibility to his family, too. He had no right to spy on her like that.

Snapping the laptop shut, she glanced around. The hidden drawer under the table was still the best place to secure the computer and photographic evidence. She slid the laptop back into the secret compartment, but before she locked the drawer and pocketed the key, she removed four of the photographs labeled *missing* and slipped them into the side pocket of her cargo pants. Then she unlocked her grandfather's gun cabinet.

She was going to see that mine for herself.

She needed to stand exactly where her grandfather had stood. She wanted to match the photos to the Sodwana site, walk Gus's last steps, *feel* what he might have felt.

The mine lay farther north, and the area was isolated. Her grandfather had taught her to go prepared when going anywhere in the Alaskan bush, so Muirinn removed a .22 rifle and a box of ammunition.

Perhaps once she'd been to the mine, she'd manage to make some sense of it all.

Jett sat at his glass-topped trestle desk, the blueprints for his wilderness lodge spread out in front of him—his big dream project. But he couldn't concentrate on his future.

He hadn't been able to concentrate at all since Muirinn O'Donnell walked back into his life.

He picked up his scopes again and went back to the window, excitement trilling dangerously like a drug though his blood. He could not get her words from yesterday out of his mind. They'd lodged inside him like a big barbed hook, bleeding a trickle of hope deep into his system.

A rueful grin tugged at his lips as he saw that she'd drawn the blinds. His smile deepened—he hadn't been able to stop himself from toying with her when she'd caught him red-handed with his binoculars aimed at her house. Locking eyes with her through those scopes had been intense, sexual, even over the distance. Damn, she'd made him hard just by looking.

It had always been that way with Muirinn. She sparked the playful in him. The daring. The lust.

The goddamn pain.

Easy on the eyes, hard on the heart—that was Muirinn O'Donnell.

And now that he knew she was available, and that she still clearly wanted him, it raised the stakes.

Big time.

He swore softly.

Going near her again would be akin to touching fire. He'd get burned, and he knew it.

Even worse, Troy would get burned.

Jett put the scopes down, and returned to his desk. But he still couldn't focus on his project. And the more he sat there, the more he felt like an ass for his little episode with the binoculars.

He grabbed his shirt, yanked on his jeans and scooped up his keys.

He drove his truck over to Muirinn's house under the pretext of apologizing for scoping her out; besides, he needed to head into the village anyway, to pick up some supplies. But deep down Jett just needed to see her again. She was his addiction; always had been.

But as he pulled into her driveway, he saw that Gus's truck was gone, and Mrs. Wilkie was bustling down the front steps of the porch, bag in hand, looking flustered.

He rolled down his window, hooked his elbow out. "Lydia?" he said.

She started. "Jett! Muirinn's not here."

He frowned at the odd edginess in her tone. "Do you know where she went?"

"That's the whole thing, Jett—she went to that awful mine! I…I told her she shouldn't go alone, but you know Muirinn. She never did listen. She left in a real hurry, and she was carrying one of Gus's guns."

"*What?* Are you sure?"

"Of course I'm sure. It was a hunting rifle."

"I mean, are you sure that she went to *Tolkin?*"

"That's where she said she was going."

Jett thought about Muirinn's suspicions—the way she'd practically interrogated Chief Moran.

Had she managed to access Gus's laptop and found out more? Is that why she'd gone to the mine?

Damn—she'd said she would call him.

Angry now, and more than a little concerned, Jett suddenly slammed his truck in reverse, sped backwards down the driveway and spun out into the dirt road.

He punched down on the gas and headed north to the abandoned mine, a sense of unease digging deeper into his chest.

Chapter 6

Muirinn sped down the dirt road, fine gray alluvial silt billowing out behind Gus's truck as she made her way up through the gulley, into the valley of the Tolkin Mine.

It felt good to drive with the window down, to have the warm summer wind ripping through her long hair, the big fat truck tires under her. The wilderness of this place was whispering through her again, awakening her consciousness.

After having lived in Manhattan, traveling the world, chasing her image of freedom, Muirinn finally realized how much she'd actually sacrificed. Deep down, she knew that everything she'd ever dreamed of was right here.

But she'd needed to get beyond those granite peaks, transcend it all, see what lay beyond the horizons just to be able to return on her own terms. When she was ready.

Except she *hadn't* come back on her own terms.

She'd come on Gus's terms—the terms of his will.

Muirinn drew up at Gate 7, the main entrance to the Tolkin property, and checked the odometer—15.4 miles since leaving home. That was how far Gus would have had to have hiked with his heart condition.

Allegedly he'd done it about a month ago—in June. The weather would very likely have been warm, maybe even hot.

She didn't buy it.

That, in turn, provoked another disturbing question—had someone brought him out here? A cab, maybe? Perhaps his truck had already been malfunctioning.

But if someone *had* dropped Gus out here, why had that person failed to come forward right away when the alarm was first raised that he was missing?

And the reason she was now heading out to the mine troubled her.

Muirinn got out of the vehicle and walked slowly up to the gate. Heat pressed down on her.

A six-foot-high, rusting, chain-link fence ran the length of the property. A hardboard sign, paint peeling, clanked against a pole in the hot breeze, fading letters proclaiming the Tolkin Mine private property, warning trespassers they would be prosecuted.

The big strike had lasted over a year. Combined with the mass homicide twenty years ago, it had resulted in severe staffing and production problems for the Tolkin Mining Corporation. Development mining—the boring of new tunnels deeper into rock in order to reach fresh veins of ore—had to be scaled back, resulting in a shortage of quality ore. And new gold mines in the north had subsequently opened, producing a far greater yield. The resultant competition had killed the Safe Harbor mine, and Tolkin had finally shut its doors seven years after the bombing.

The property had sat abandoned ever since, crumbling with time and seasons.

For a moment Muirinn just stood there, snared by a surge of memories, the place coming to life with people, frantic, milling around like ants. She could hear sirens, see the acrid smoke boiling up out of D-shaft, feel the spring snow cold on her cheeks, her mother's hand icy in hers. Chief Bill Moran was walking toward them…

Clouds began to gather in the sky, suddenly darkening the ground. The air grew hotter, closer. The strange thrum of a grouse reverberated against the stillness.

Muirinn shook herself, rubbing the chill of the memory from her arms.

She glanced up at the avalanche-scarred mountains that soared up on either side of the Tolkin Valley. Their plunging chutes looked dark and ominous, although they shouldn't. They were choked with the vibrant green of deciduous summer growth that had burst from snow-scoured ground, and higher up on the peaks, avalanche lilies—a favorite food of grizzlies—had formed a verdant green carpet.

Muirinn stepped up to the gate.

The chain and lock had long ago been rusted and pried open by vandals. Unhooking what was left of the chain, Muirinn creaked open the massive gate, dragging it wide through the dirt so she could bring the truck in.

She drove through, shut the gate behind her, and traveled along the perimeter fence for about three miles until the Sodwana headframe loomed on a rise ahead, a grim, rusting, metal skeleton in the shape of an *A,* a small derelict building squatting at its base.

Just like the photo.

Muirinn stopped alongside the shed.

The windows were partially boarded up, a metal drum and old iron boxcar resting outside. Plastic flapped in the hot breeze. Her mouth felt dry.

This was a bad place, choked with the ghosts of old miners. She didn't like to think of Gus here, alone. Or down the shaft.

Muirinn retrieved the rifle from the gun box, loaded it and released the safety. She couldn't say why exactly. But she felt edgy, as if she were being watched by unseen eyes.

Wind gusted, stirring fine silt up into a soft dervish, and suddenly it was cold again, and the silt was blowing snow, and she could see Chief Bill Moran coming, looming, the grim news carried in his posture and stride... Disconcerted, Muirinn again shook away the haunting images.

This place had an eerie way of slamming present and past together, and Muirinn realized that that was exactly why Gus had come here. And why she was here now, too.

Approaching the old headframe building, the .22 clutched a little too tightly in her hand, her eyes tracked over the dry ground, trying to see where the old photos might have been taken, where some accomplice might have stood vigil on a cold morning twenty years ago as a killer trekked deep underground.

A sudden soft whoosh of breeze rustled through the alders, leaves clapping like little hands, an invisible audience watching, waiting, cheering. She glanced nervously back at the main gate. It suddenly seemed so far. Her hand touched her belly.

Maybe she shouldn't have come out here alone, but she honestly didn't know who she could turn to right now, apart from Jett. And that definitely wasn't going to happen.

Making sure her cell phone was easily accessible in her pocket, Muirinn pushed open the old door. It released an inhuman groan of protest, rusted metal grinding against the hinge.

Her heart hammered.

It was stifling inside, rank. She shivered again. Her gaze skimmed around the interior, settling on the heavy-looking grate covering the man-way as the last words in Gus's notes sifted into Muirinn's mind.

Did bomber use Sodwana shaft to access D-shaft where bomb was planted? Did accomplice stand guard at headframe?

Was that why he dragged the grate back and climbed down into that black hole?

Maybe he'd wanted to see if it was actually possible to access the bomb site underground from this shaft, and how long it might take.

No, that was pure insanity.

Her grandfather might have been eccentric, but he would never have gone down that shaft alone, not at his age, not with his heart condition. Not without telling anyone where he was going.

She propped her rifle against the wall, bent down to tug the grate off the man-way. It was heavy iron, virtually immovable. She tried to imagine Gus doing this. Sweat prickled over her body as she hefted it a few inches, then a few more, metal grating across metal until she managed to pull the grate right off. Her hands burned, smelled of rust. She'd never have gotten this off if it hadn't been removed and replaced recently.

Dank air from deep in the bowels of the earth reached up, cold, crawling right into her. Peering cautiously down into the black abyss, Muirinn was suddenly 100 percent convinced that Gus wouldn't have taken hold of the decaying old ladder rungs and climbed into that black maw alone.

But as she bent down to replace the cover, a powerful crack resounded through the quiet hills, and a slug slammed into metal just near her shoulder. A cloud of birds scattered from a clump of alders.

It took a nanosecond for Muirinn to grasp what had just happened.

Gunshot!

She crouched down, mind racing. *Must be a hunter. And I just happen to be in the line of fire,* she thought, peeking up carefully through the slatted boards just as another explosive sound boomed through the valley. A slug hammered into the opposite wall, splitting a support beam into shrapnel. A piece stabbed into her shoulder.

Muirinn gasped, clamping her hand over the wound. Blood started to well between her fingers, dribbling down her arm. The report echoed down through the valley, fading into the distant stillness.

She could hardly breathe.

That was no simple rifle. That was the distinctive explosive sound of a point three-effing-oh-three, with enough firepower to fell a moose at full charge!

Almost immediately, another shot walloped through the wall. She dived to her knees, slamming down onto her side into the dirt. Her phone clattered out of her pocket and skittered across the floor.

Grouse fluttered outside.

Someone was shooting at this shack!

She lay dead still, heart jackhammering, skin drenched with sweat. And blood.

Then came another report—this one clunking off the ironwork outside.

Her stomach started to cramp. *My baby.* Oh, Lord, she shouldn't have come here alone. Muirinn inched along the dirt on her side, reaching for her rifle. Gripping it in her hands, she wriggled over to a second window that had been boarded over. She edged up, inserted the barrel of her .22 through a large crack. She scanned the mountainside with her scopes, trying to locate the shooter.

She caught a movement in the brush, a slight glint of sunlight against metal. Someone was hiding in the bush, dressed in camo gear and hunting cap, aiming at the shed.

With shaking hands she snugged her cheek against the stock, aimed to the right of the sniper and slowly squeezed off a round.

Almost instantly the sniper returned fire, blasting the boards clear from the window. Muirinn screamed, dropping her rifle as she scrambled for cover. Shattered wood blew clear across the room, a piece glancing across her temple.

Panic and pain tore through her body.

Her weapon was no match for that kind of firepower.

Muirinn tried to crawl over to her phone. But the sniper could now see in through the window with his powerful scope, and a slug *thwoked* into the dirt just in front of her cell, shooting sand into her face.

She lurched back with a whimper, crawled into a far corner and cowered there, blood now running down her face from the wound on her temple as more slugs slammed through the shack.

The only reason she wasn't dead already was because the heavy metal boxcar outside was preventing bullets from coming through the wall. But that meant she couldn't move. She couldn't call for help.

Tears of frustration burned into her eyes. She held her stomach, feeling small cramps sparking across her abdomen.

Oh, please, I don't want to die like this. I don't want to lose my baby.

Then she heard a slug thunk into her truck outside, and the powerful odor of gas fumes reached her nostrils. Another well-aimed shot ignited the fuel with an explosive *whoosh* that filled the air with a rush. She heard the hot crackle of flames, saw black smoke rising outside the far window. Someone out there was determined to kill her.

If the shack caught fire, she'd be burned alive.

If she tried to flee, she'd be shot.

She was trapped.

Jett's truck bounced over ruts in the road as he raced north, a cone of silt roiling out behind him. His gun lay on the seat beside him. He had no idea what Muirinn was up to, but a cold instinct told him trouble awaited.

Nearing the Tolkin perimeter, he saw a plume of black smoke twisting up into the wind.

Jett slammed down on the gas and blew his truck right through the closed mine gate, smashing it back with a violent crash and scrape of metal. Spinning his tires in the fine dry dirt, he swerved and sped along the perimeter fence, aiming for the source of the smoke.

As he approached, he realized it was Gus's red truck burning.

Jett drove even faster. But suddenly a cloud of dirt spat sharply up in front of his tires. Then another. Then something thudded into the bed of his truck.

With raw, gut-slamming shock, Jett realized that someone up in the hills was shooting at *him,* trying to stop him from reaching the shed. And judging by the burning wreck of the truck and the state of the shed, Muirinn was holed up in there like prey.

Or worse.

She could already be dead.

Chapter 7

Jett skidded to a stop behind the headframe building and flung open his door, dropping down behind his vehicle as another shot slammed into the ground. Resting his rifle barrel on the bed of the truck, Jett edged up, squinting into the scope.

He saw the glint of a weapon, then a sharp movement in leaves up on the hill, as if the sniper had suddenly seen him looking and ducked.

Reining in his adrenaline, Jett forced his breath out, slow and measured, and he squeezed off a shot. The bushes on the hill rustled sharply. Then a cloud of dust boiled up into the air as the shooter fled into the mountains on an all-terrain vehicle.

Jett burst through the shed door, slamming it back off its hinge.

Muirinn scampered backwards with a whimper, blind terror in her eyes as she cowered into a tight ball in the corner. Blood and tears streaked her sheet-white face.

A terrible fear gripped Jett as he dropped to his knees, rifle to the ground as reached for her. "*Muirinn!* How badly are you hurt?"

She sagged visibly as she registered his voice. "Oh, God, Jett—"

He took her quickly into his arms, her entire body trembling like a frail aspen branch. He held her tight and she sobbed, releasing everything, giving herself fully over to him, to his care. To his embrace. And it tore into his soul. He wrapped his arms more tightly around her, a fierce, raw rage bubbling inside him.

He fought to tamp it down. Uncontrolled aggression bred rash decisions.

He needed cool.

Focus.

Jett blinked back his hot emotion and stroked her hair back from her face. "What in hell happened here?" he said, examining the cut on her temple.

She couldn't talk. Not yet. Sobs still wracked her body, choking her words.

"Shhh, it's okay," he whispered. "It's just a surface wound. But they do bleed a lot." He removed his hunting knife from the sheath on his belt and used the tip to tear back the bloodsoaked sleeve from her shoulder.

"Got some wood fragments in there. I have a first aid kit in the truck, but we need to get out into the light." He helped her to her feet and led her from the shed. Coughing, eyes burning from toxic black smoke, they steered clear of Gus's smoldering vehicle.

Once they were well away from the mine property, Jett pulled over onto the side of the road and tended to Muirinn as she sat in the passenger seat, feet hanging out the door.

Putting his paramedic training to work, he cleansed the wound on her brow then applied a butterfly suture just under her hairline.

"A stitch or three and you'll be as good as new," he reassured her gently. But he had to force his voice to stay level, because inside his belly trembled with raw protective rage, and it took every ounce of control to bottle it in. He was angry with her, too, for coming out here alone.

"What happened here, Muirinn?" he asked softly as he pulled the shard from her shoulder, feeling her wince as he did. "What were you doing at the mine?" He taped the wound tightly shut, noting the ripped knees on her dust-caked pants, the deathly pallor of her complexion. His chest tightened.

"I wanted to see where Gus was found." Her voice sounded small, scared.

"I swear that idiot was trying to kill me. I thought it was over. I…I thought I was going to die, Jett. You…" her voice hitched. "You gave me—my baby—a second chance. I can't tell you how grateful I am." Tears tracked down through the dirt on her face.

He stilled his hand against her cheek.

A second chance. Was it possible for them? Could they ever try again?

He felt his body—every molecule in his system—aching to kiss her, hold her, comfort her. And Jett started to shake against his restraint, the powerful aftereffects of the massive cortisol dump to his system finally seizing control. With it his anger mushroomed.

"You shouldn't have come out here alone, Muirinn," he said brusquely.

Her mouth flattened at his admonition.

He grabbed his phone. "I'm calling the cops."

"No! Wait!" She clamped her hand on his arm, looking mortified.

"What for?"

She closed her eyes for a moment, sucking in air deeply, bolstering herself. "Gus's death wasn't an accident, Jett."

"What are you saying? Did you get into his laptop? Did you find something?"

She nodded. "Gus had new evidence on the Tolkin homicide, something that could lead to the bomber. I think he was murdered because of it, and whoever killed him might believe that *I* have seen it, and now they might be trying to silence *me*."

"Why in hell didn't you come to me with this first, Muirinn, before charging off half cocked to the mine?"

She sighed heavily, limbs still trembling, and guilt pinged through Jett. He knew why.

Muirinn was avoiding him because he hadn't been able to come clean on his divorce. She was staying away out of respect for him.

He softened his voice. "Tell me what was in those files, Muirinn."

"Ike Potter, a retired cop who worked for the SHPD at the time of the Tolkin homicide apparently gave Gus some old crime scene photographs—"

"I knew Ike. He had cancer, passed away just two months—"

"Yes," she interjected. "And just before he died, he handed Gus information from the old Tolkin investigation. Evidence that had been buried by the SHPD, never making it into the hands of the FBI team."

"What?"

"Hear me out." Her eyes looked glassy. She was going into

shock—pale, clammy skin, breathing too fast and light. Jett was worried about her baby.

"Muirinn, listen, we need to get you checked out. You can finishing telling me all this on the way to—"

"No! Listen to me first, Jett, please!" She grasped his hands. "You need to know this *before* we figure out who we can talk to." She swallowed hard, glancing nervously toward the mountains into which the shooter had fled. "Among the missing crime scene photos were shots of two different sets of boot prints. One set of prints was made inside and outside the Sodwana headframe on the morning of the bombing. It appears the bomber had an accomplice, Jett, someone who waited at the headframe while the bomber climbed down the shaft—"

"That shaft is *miles* away from the bomb site, Muirinn. I don't even know if the bomb site *is* accessible from Sodwana."

"I don't know, either, and maybe that's what Gus was trying to find out. But the FBI was never given those photographs, Jett. And apparently the tracks themselves were obliterated by someone on the SHPD force before the postblast team could get in. The FBI never explored that angle because there was no evidence to corroborate it."

Jett shook his head. "Muirinn, this doesn't make sense. Why would Ike have sat on this information all these years? And why suddenly hand it over to Gus?"

"Because he was dying, Jett, and he wanted to come clean. Because he was a cop, and he'd been eaten up by guilt these past twenty years. Maybe Ike sat on the evidence because he was a rookie at the time of the blast, and he was afraid of ratting out a superior officer—someone who could still be around now." She gripped his hands tighter in her urgency to get her message across.

"Gus probably felt secure in thinking that no one knew

what Ike had given him, Jett. But someone *must* have found out, someone who is still trying to keep the past buried. And will kill to do so."

Jett leaned back in shock. "So you think Gus was *murdered?*"

She hesitated, suddenly growing more pale, exhausted, drained. She glanced in the direction of the mine. "I *know* he was," she whispered. "After looking down that hole I know in my heart that my grandfather would never have gone down there on his own. Something bad happened to him."

"Muirinn," he said gently. "Your grandfather was known for his eccentricity, his obsession with Tolkin. And remember that both the ME and Gus's doctor were in agreement about the cause of his death. The police didn't voice any suspicions about foul play, either."

"The *police?* Listen to yourself, Jett! It was someone on that same police force who helped sabotage an FBI investigation into a mass murder, and who let a killer walk free. This is a conspiracy."

Jett rubbed his brow. He couldn't deny that someone had been taking serious potshots at Muirinn, and at him. And he'd seen someone in camo gear flee north into the wilderness.

The seriousness of her allegation bored more deeply into him. Along with it came an ominous chill.

Muirinn gasped suddenly, clutching at her stomach. Jett's heart lurched and he reached for her. But she shook her head, smiling wanly. "It's just kicking again," she whispered, awe filling her incredible eyes. She grasped his hand quickly. "Here, feel." She placed his palm on her belly.

Tears burned into Jett's eyes as he felt her child moving. He looked up into Muirinn's face, a sense of wonder rippling through his body. She met his gaze, and together they felt her baby move again, rolling over in her womb, and a powerful, sensual bond shuddered between them.

Jett's breathing quickened.

This was the exact privilege she'd denied him when she was pregnant with Troy. Now she was denying some other man this same sense of wonder.

Anger surged afresh through Jett, his grip on control cracking at the thought of just how close she and this little baby had come to getting killed—at the pain the father who'd sired this child would feel upon receiving news of his baby's death, regardless of whether or not he was still seeing Muirinn.

"Get in the truck," he said crisply, trying to hide his own emotions. "I'm taking you straight to Dr. Callaghan. She knows what she's doing. She's delivered tons of babies, and she's Troy's doctor."

"I'm fine, really."

"It's not you I'm worried about, Muirinn. It's your baby." Jett's words came out far harsher than he intended, but he couldn't stop himself. "You had no right going out there if you knew your life would be threatened."

He went around to the driver's side, got in, slammed the door and rammed his truck into gear. "Buckle up." He fired the ignition.

"I didn't *know* I was in danger, Jett. Not until I was shot at. I was still piecing together—"

"Oh, so you just brought that .22 with you for fun?" He hit the gas, fishtailing back onto the dirt road, taking his frustrations out on the truck. "What were you expecting—a bit of hunting along the way? I know you, Muirinn. You think you can go playing Nancy Drew without considering—"

"You know *nothing* about me, Jett!" she snapped. "You're talking about someone you last saw a decade ago."

The truth sobered him, made his eyes cool, his heart hard. His jaw tight. "You might be doing this baby gig on your own, Muirinn," he said very quietly, hands gripping the wheel tightly. "But somewhere out there is still a father who might just give a damn that his kid actually lives! You were always so damn selfish, O'Donnell."

"What is this really about, Jett?" she said quietly. "What are you really trying to say to me?"

That you gave our son away without thinking of me, and that you still haven't told me the truth.

"All you ever think about is yourself, Muirinn."

She stared at him in silence, blood beginning to trickle out from under the butterfly suture on her brow. Jett drove faster, knuckles white on the wheel.

"There is no man, Jett," she said softly.

His head swiveled. "What?"

"There is no father. I did this in a doctor's office. With sperm from a donor bank. Artificial insemination, Jett. Just me. Solo."

He stared at her in shock.

"Watch out!"

He swerved, just missing a tree on a bend, and slammed on the brakes, the vehicle sliding to a stop on the grit-covered road. He turned off the engine.

Dust settled quietly around the truck. He could hear the soft rush of wind in conifers outside, feel the cooler air against his face.

"God, I'm sorry." He dragged his hands over his hair. "I was just so worried about you, about your baby, Muirinn."

She looked out the window, avoiding his eyes.

He swore softly at his idiocy. "Why?" he said quietly. "Why'd you do it?"

"I want a child." She turned to face him, fresh tears and old mascara tracking down the dirt on her pale cheeks. Her hair was a matted mess of dried blood and silt. But she'd never looked more beautiful to him. *Or more available.*

"I want a family, Jett. I want to be a mother. What's so wrong with that? And I couldn't find the right man—a man who'd want to do this with me. So I'm doing it alone."

She really was totally free.

And she wanted all those things that he'd wanted from her all those years ago. All that wasted time suddenly yawned out in front of him. Jett didn't trust himself to speak.

Instead, he turned on the ignition.

As he drove, he tried to process everything she'd said, and a humming started in his muscles, his whole body soon vibrating like a tuning fork.

A second chance.

Was it really possible?

What would it take to get there? It would take Muirinn telling him about the boy she'd given up for adoption, that's what—that was Jett's line in the sand. He *needed* to hear this in order to find a way to tell her about Troy.

And before Jett could tell Troy that Kim was not his mom, Jett needed to be damn sure that Muirinn was committed, that she was going to stay right here in Safe Harbor, and be here for their son.

He gripped the wheel more tightly, the possibilities suddenly so frighteningly fragile inside him. But the excitement wasn't without remorse, because Muirinn could have a family eleven years ago.

With him.

Whatever move he made now, Jett told himself, his son had to come first. He owed that to his boy. Because just as easily as Muirinn had thrown it all away the first time, she had the power to do it again.

Chapter 8

Jett paced like a caged bear in Dr. Pat Callaghan's waiting room. He'd brought Muirinn straight here instead of taking her to the hospital because he trusted Pat. Her specialty was obstetrics and her office was rigged for ultrasound.

She'd also taken excellent care of Troy when Jett had first brought his tiny infant son home to Safe Harbor, feeling nervous about being a new dad at the tender age of twenty-two.

The exam room door opened suddenly, and Jett spun around.

A band clamped tightly over his chest as he saw Muirinn's wan face, the neat little plaster over the fresh stitches on her forehead, the bandage on her shoulder under her ripped shirt.

But despite her trauma, there appeared to be a subtle new determination in her stride as she exited the exam room with the doctor. Pat smiled, nodding to Jett as she picked up a clipboard and pen. "We just need to fill out some paperwork and mom and daughter are good to go."

Daughter?

Jett's heart stalled.

He could barely focus on the doctor's next words. "I had your grandfather on Digoxin, Muirinn." She filled in a form as she spoke. "It's a generic digitalis preparation."

"Could an overdose have possibly caused his cardiac arrest?"

Pat's pen stilled, and she looked up. "Well, yes. But—"

"Either way the ME would have expected to find digitalis in his system, right?"

"Yes, he would. But the ME's involvement in Gus's case was a formality, really, because the cause of death was clear, especially given Gus's preexisting condition—"

Muirinn interrupted. "Does it honestly make sense to you, Dr. Callaghan, that my grandfather hiked all the way out to Tolkin with his heart condition, and then climbed all the way down that shaft? I mean…" she hesitated. "Everyone keeps reminding me that he was eccentric. But I need to know, in your professional opinion, was my grandfather of sound mind these last couple of months?"

Dr. Callaghan placed a hand on Muirinn's arm, and smiled comfortingly. "It's always tough to lose someone, Muirinn. But I can assure you that Gus was mentally agile, if somewhat creative in thought. Plus he'd started taking daily walks on my recommendation, so he might easily have included the Tolkin property along one of his routes."

"It's fifteen miles from his house. I clocked it on the odometer."

The doctor returned to filling in her form. "That's really not far for a good hike if you take it slow, you know." She set the clipboard down. "Your grandfather had a really good life, Muirinn. He died active, busy. Not tied to a wheelchair, not in a hospital bed. Gus wouldn't have wanted it any other way."

"I know." She glanced down. "It's just that…I guess I was wondering, given the unusual circumstances."

"I don't believe the circumstances were that unusual, especially knowing your grandfather. Gus had always been obsessed with that mine, almost pathologically fixated, in my opinion. Both the ME and I were satisfied, upon examining his body, that it was the heart condition that caused his death, and resulted in a small tumble. This is not unusual in cardiac arrest."

"He was down a mine shaft."

"And according to the police, there was absolutely no sign of foul play. He'd simply been poking around there when he collapsed."

Muirinn shot Jett a glance.

The doctor smiled again, compassion fanning out in warm crinkles from her hazel eyes. "Now go and get some rest, Muirinn. Take care of that baby girl of yours."

"Thank you, doctor."

Jett swallowed against the dryness in his throat, the thought of what they could have shared eleven years ago suddenly so stark, as he led Muirinn out into the street, back to his truck.

"Did you tell the doc what happened at the mine?" he said, holding open the passenger door.

"No, I just told her I was out for a walk, and that I slipped and fell down a bank." She hesitated. "Doesn't it strike you as strange that Gus's case was basically rubber-stamped by the ME?"

"No, it doesn't." He went around, climbed in the driver's side and started the engine. "From Pat's point of view, what she said makes sense, Muirinn."

"Well, I think the ME should have done a more in-depth investigation, and done toxicology tests…something."

"Are you saying you don't trust Doc Callaghan and the ME now, either?"

She strapped herself in. "I'm just trying to figure out what in hell happened, Jett."

Jett pulled out into the small main road. "Why were you asking about Gus's medication?"

"I was wondering if he might have been poisoned. Technically, a heart attack could have been induced using Gus's own meds, in an effort to make his death seem as if it were from natural causes."

Jett focused on the road ahead thinking how absurd it seemed to be having this conversation at all. He was still trying to wrap his head around the fact that Muirinn had almost been killed, and that they couldn't go to the police with this information.

One way or another the cops *were* going to find Gus's burned-out truck at the mine, and questions were going to be asked.

This was going to come out somehow.

Bitterness leached down his throat as he thought of the historic blast, and what it had done to this town. He tried to imagine how much that bomber and his accomplice might stand to lose now, if the truth came out that they were responsible for one of the biggest mass homicides north of 60.

Who *wouldn't* kill to keep something like that quiet?

"We need to get to the bottom of this, Muirinn," he said quietly as he drove. "You need to show me those photographs, and Gus's notes."

"I don't want to involve you, Jett," she said with a heavy sigh.

"I can't let you do this on your own, Muirinn. Not now."

She sat in silence. He could sense the nervous tension rolling off her in waves.

He cursed to himself.

He didn't want this any more than she did. What he needed was some distance between Muirinn and himself, so he could try to figure some things out. Everything was moving too fast, and he was scared of what it might do to all of them.

But he was also the only one who could protect her right now.

The only emotional barrier he had left was the fact that Muirinn thought he was married. And the more he was forced into her proximity, the harder that secret was going to be to keep.

But, damn, he *needed* to keep it right now. It was the only way he'd be able to keep his hands off her.

They drove in tense silence along the twisting coast road, the late evening sun turning the ocean into beaten copper.

"Is it really a girl?" he said suddenly, thinking again that the child had no father.

Muirinn nodded as she placed her hands on her tummy. "I wanted it to be surprise, but after being in that shed, convinced I was going to die…" She inhaled shakily. "When Dr. Callaghan gave me an ultrasound just to check that everything was okay, she asked if I knew the sex, or if wanted to know. I said yes."

"You happy?"

"I am. I…I've always wanted a daughter."

"What about a son?" There was something in the tone of his voice that made Muirinn glance at him.

But Jett didn't return the look, and she couldn't read his eyes. Yet his hands had tightened on the wheel, and his neck was tense. She studied the lines of his rugged profile, his thick dark hair, his strong arms. And she loved him all over again. Age had been good to him. She wondered what might have been if she hadn't left, if they'd raised the boy she gave away for adoption. Guilt and confusion twisted inside Muirinn like a knife.

She was suddenly overwhelmed by a desperate desire to open up, spill everything about the fact she'd had a son—*their son*—that she'd given him away. But it was all too much to handle right now. A part of Muirinn even wondered if was better that Jett didn't know.

He had his own family now, and she didn't want to tamper with that.

The other part of her was afraid of how much he might truly hate her if she told him all these years later.

"Yes," she whispered, remorse thickening her voice. "I wanted a son, too."

He turned into her driveway, came to a stop and sat silent for a several beats, staring out the windshield. Then his gaze flashed to her, fierce suddenly. "Look, I can't let you stay here alone, Muirinn. Not after what happened today. You need to pack a bag and stay at my place until...until we've figured this out."

Fear, anxiety, attraction erupted in a dangerous cocktail inside Muirinn. She could *not* be forced into such close proximity to this married man, alone with him in his house, his wife away. "I...I don't think that's a good idea, Jett." Her voice caught, turning husky as his eyes bored hotly into hers, the intense stare of a hunter. Anticipation rustled through Muirinn like a wild and lethal thing.

She swallowed. "I just can't do it. I...cannot be with you, not in your house...I still have..."

"Still have what, Muirinn?" His voice was low, gravelly, his gaze drifting down to her lips.

"You know that I still have feelings for you, Jett," she whispered.

His eyes darkened, and lust etched into his face. Heat arrowed through her body, her world swirling to a narrow focus, logic fleeing.

Jett raised his hand to touch her face. He wanted her. To feel her hair, her skin, her body wrapped around his. But he couldn't go down this road again. Not yet, not before both of them had confessed the secrets between them. He exhaled slowly, lowering his hand.

Her body sagged visibly at his rejection, and her eyes glistened sharply with hurt. The pulse in her neck was racing, the emotion in her face so raw. "Muirinn, I—"

He just couldn't stop what came next. Cupping her jaw, Jett bent down, sliding his hand under her hair and he lowered his mouth to hers. His heart pounded as his lips met hers. There was no rational thought at all, as he felt her mouth open under his.

A small sound came from her throat as his tongue entered her mouth. She kissed him back, hard, desperate. And he felt the wetness of tears against his skin.

She hooked her arms around his neck, drawing him closer, her tongue tangling with his as she melted into him. Jett felt her pregnant body press against his, and something inside him cracked. His body burned as he kissed her harder, deeper. And they moved faster—urgent, hungry, angry, digging down deep for something neither of them seemed to be able to reach in the other.

Jett pulled back suddenly, rocked, breathing hard.

Muirinn stared at him in wide-eyed shock, chest rising and falling fast, cheeks flushed, panic flickering in her features.

Her hand covered her mouth, horror dawning in her eyes at the reality of what had just happened.

He didn't say a word, didn't move. *Couldn't.*

"Jett…" Tears streamed fresh down her face. She turned suddenly, flung open the door, slammed it shut, and stumbled up the stairs to her house.

Chapter 9

Muirinn's hands were shaking too hard to get the key into the lock.

Jett's truck door banged behind her. She heard his footsteps crunching on gravel, heard him coming up the stairs. She wanted to sink into the floor, be swallowed by a hole.

He stilled her hand, took the key from her and opened her front door. "I'm sorry," he said quietly, holding the door open. "It won't happen again. Please, just get your things, Muirinn," he said. "I'll wait for you downstairs."

She clenched her jaw. "I'm not coming to your house, Jett."

"Then I'll stay at your place," he said, following her into the hallway. "But it'll be easier the other way. I have my work at home."

She spun around to face him. "I never wanted to put you in this position, Jett. I didn't—*don't*—want your help." *Just as she hadn't let him help her eleven years ago when she found out she was pregnant.*

He let out a wry laugh. "You never did let anyone help you, Muirinn. You always wanted to do everything on your own. Let me help you now. For the baby's sake."

"I *can't*," she whispered.

"Look, I really am sorry about what just happened, and if I could find someone I trust to stay with you tonight, Muirinn, I would. And after tomorrow, if things still haven't been sorted out, I have a good friend who will do me that favor."

A favor.

Pain twisted.

That was the last thing on this earth she wanted from Jett. "So why don't you get him now?" she said icily.

"He's away until tomorrow."

She swallowed, humiliation filling her chest. She'd led him to this—it was as much her fault as his—and now she just wanted to be alone, in her old bedroom where she could sob her heart out. And he wasn't going to let her do that.

"Please, Jett," she said, clenching her jaw, refusing to let him see her break down further. "Please get out of my house. Now."

Frustration flashed into his cobalt eyes. "Someone just tried to kill you, Muirinn. I can't leave you here alone. As soon as possible I'll get my buddy Hamilton Brock to come stay here with you. He's an ex-Marine and does close protection work for a private company offshore. He knows what he's doing."

She turned away from him, rested her forehead against the doorjamb, shoulders slumping with fatigue. She just couldn't stay in Jett's house with his wife away. It wasn't right. It wasn't helping either of them. God, this was a mess.

"Think of your child for a change, Muirinn."

Her head whipped up. "For a *change?*"

"Yes. Someone other than yourself for a change."

"Damn you, Rutledge," she whispered, eyes blurring with tears she could no longer force back. "Will you get off your high horse! I didn't *ask* you to kiss me back there! What about *your* responsibilities—to your family, to your *son?*"

His body went rigid.

She swore softly. "The best thing I ever did was leave you and this place."

"That's in the past, this is—"

"Oh, it might be in the past, Jett, but what just happened in that truck has *everything* to do with now."

His jaw flexed angrily. He stuffed his hands into his pockets. "Muirinn, please, just get your things. Bring the photographs and laptop. We'll go through it all, and we can decide where to go from there, whether there is enough to bring in an outside agency like the FBI. You can shower and change at my place." He hesitated. "Just for tonight. At least you'll be safe."

Safe?

That's the last thing she was with Jett. Her own heart had made sure of that. *He* had made sure of that. She turned, stomped up the stairs, slamming doors behind her.

So she was angry with him. Well, he was angry with himself. Jett slammed his fist against the wall.

A door banged upstairs.

He dragged both hands over his hair and cursed. *Idiot!* He should never should never have touched her. But it had just happened.

He swore again.

What else was he supposed to do now? They couldn't go to the cops. And he didn't know who else to trust, apart from Brock, who'd arrived in town only seven years ago and had no connections whatsoever to the Tolkin blast.

All Jett had to do was keep his hands off her for maybe forty-eight hours, max, until he could reach Brock. But the more he was with Muirinn, the more he wanted her. And the longer he tried brush the fact that he was divorced under the carpet, the more onerous the deception became, and the worse it was going to be to tell the truth.

Not to mention the truth about Troy.

Her words sifted into his mind: *"I wanted a son, too."*

Well, she could have damn well had one if she hadn't given him up for adoption, right? He stalked across the living room, furious with himself and his own out-of-control libido.

Gus's silver tomcat watched Jett as he paced, its tail flicking like an irritating metronome. He scowled at the creature, then strode into the kitchen, looking at Gus's things, anything to distract himself while he waited.

He picked up a small tin of herb tea, prepared by Mrs. Wilkie, no doubt. The label said *comfrey*. He opened the tin, shook the thin furry dried leaves, put it back, then picked up another tin. Chamomile. He set it back, stared at the foxglove bells in a copper vase on the long wooden table, the basket of vegetables in the kitchen. Mrs. Wilkie was still doing her thing, as if Gus were still here, as if nothing had changed.

But so much had changed—the echoes from a murderous blast two decades ago still rippling into the future.

Jett felt bad for the old woman. Gus had always been good to her, and he knew Lydia Wilkie was deeply fond of him.

If Muirinn was correct—if Gus *had* been murdered—Jett was going to make damn sure the bastard paid, and that an end was finally put to this case. He stalked back through the living room.

There were photos and paintings of Muirinn everywhere.

Claustrophobia reared up and came down on him with sharp teeth bared. He swung around, feeling short of breath.

And there she was.

Standing in the brick archway with her bag in hand, her ripped pants still caked with silt from the mine, her hair still matted. Gone was the feisty redhead. She looked more like a forlorn orphan.

"I need to leave a note for Mrs. Wilkie to feed the cat," she said stiffly.

"Fine."

She got a notepad from the hall table, her movements tense, mouth tight. She'd been crying again. God, he felt bad, putting her through the ringer after all she'd gone through today. He had no right to kiss her, and here he was telling her that she needed to think of something other than herself, while he'd acted like a selfish ass. What must she think of him?

"Muirinn... I... "

She looked up.

I'm not married. And I still love you.

He clamped his mouth shut.

She returned her attention to scribbling a note for Mrs. Wilkie, purple petals falling onto the back of her pale hand as she inserted the corner of the paper under the big copper vase on the table. She removed a key from her pocket and unlocked a drawer hidden into the side of the table. And gasped, hand flying to her mouth.

"Muirinn, what is it?"

Her eyes flared to his, panic on her face.

"It's gone! The laptop—it's *missing!*" She rummaged frantically. "The envelope with the photos—that's gone, too!"

She yanked the drawer out further.

"Maybe you put the laptop somewhere else?"

"No, Jett! It was *here*. All the evidence is *gone*..." Her eyes flickered as she remembered something. "Except for these—" She fumbled to unbutton the side pocket of her cargo pants.

With a shaking hand she held out a set of crumpled black-and-whites. "I took these four photos with me to the mine so I could compare them with the area around the Sodwana shaft."

He placed his hand over hers, stopping the shaking. "Come," he said firmly. "I'm taking you home. We can think about this later."

Jett handed Muirinn her bag as they entered the hallway of his house. "I'll set up the spare room for you," he said. "Bathroom's that way."

She walked slowly into the living room, bag in hand. Pale evening sunlight slatted through skylights in a high, vaulted ceiling, and windows overlooking the sea yawned up from natural wood floors—Jett's love affair with the sky evident in the renovations he had made to his parents' old home.

"Are you absolutely sure you didn't put that laptop somewhere else?" he asked as he walked into his kitchen.

"Of course I'm sure." She took in the décor as she spoke. Mounted photographs graced his living room walls—aerial shots of caribou racing across a frozen tundra below the wingtip of a plane, black-and-white images of antique airplanes, family pictures. Muirinn stalled suddenly in front of a photo of Jett and his son, Troy in the cockpit of a small plane.

Her throat closed in on itself.

Troy looked so much like his father; smoky dark lashes, ink-black hair, bright white teeth in a broad smile. But his eyes were green, and he had a slight smattering of freckles across his sun-browned cheeks.

He was around the same age her son would be now— *their* son.

The thought stung.

Slowly, she turned her attention to another photo, this one of Jett, Kim and Troy on Jett's boat. Kim was beautiful— blond with pale blue eyes. Jett had his arms around both his wife and child. The family vignette made Muirinn flinch.

She could feel Jett watching her from the kitchen entrance, silent.

Tearing her attention away from the photos, Muirinn made her way to the bathroom, forcing herself not to look back at him.

While Muirinn was bathing, Jett warmed soup he'd made with vegetables from his garden and caribou he'd shot last August. He struggled to concentrate on the task at hand, and not think of Muirinn naked and pregnant in his bathtub, in his home.

Back in his life after all these years.

He heard her come out of the bathroom and head into the spare room. He buttered some toast and dished the soup into bowls, the sensation of her mouth, her taste, her kiss curling back into his mind as he watched the steam.

He carried the plates out and put them on the low coffee table in front of the sofa, then went to his drafting table and quickly began rolling up his blueprints. He didn't want her to see them, didn't want her asking about his life, his future. His big dream.

He needed to stay focused on just getting her through whatever in hell was going on—and keeping himself from getting too close.

"What are those?" she said appearing in the doorway.

He tensed. "Just some plans for a wilderness lodge I'm building farther up north."

"Where up north?" She came closer, toweling her hair, wearing soft sweats, her scent clean, soapy.

He didn't answer the question. "Soup's on the table."

Muirinn padded softly into the living room and sat on the sofa, tucking her feet under her.

She ate while Jett studied the four crumpled photos she'd given him.

"Good soup," she said.

He glanced up. Color was returning to her cheeks. Relief washed softly through him. "Tell me again what Gus wrote in his laptop about these," he said, positioning the photos next to each other on the coffee table.

"Those four images were among the photos allegedly removed from police evidence before the arrival of the FBI postblast team. That one—" she pointed with her spoon, "—shows bootprints outside the Sodwana headframe building. Apparently, those were left by the bomber's accomplice."

He looked up, catching her eyes, and the memory of their kiss shimmered between them. Her cheeks flushed and she cleared her throat, returning her attention to the photos. "And those two sets of tracks in the dark mud were apparently left by the bomber himself."

Jett tapped a photo with his finger. "The ruler next to the prints outside the Sodwana shaft indicates that the accomplice wore a size 12 boot. I figure the print up in Gus's attic was also a size 12."

Muirinn set her bowl down and rubbed her arms, as if she were cold suddenly. "You think it was actually the *same* guy who broke into my house?"

"Hell knows. The ruler next to these other prints in the darker mud shows that the bomber wore a size 10 boot." He frowned slowly as he studied the photo more closely.

"They're odd tracks," he said, a whisper of unspecified foreboding rustling down his spine. "It looks like the guy was dragging one foot, or something."

She nodded, watching him intently.

"What else did Gus say about these prints, Muirinn?"

"That's all. His notes just ended in midstream."

"Did he have a theory about *who* might have left these tracks?"

"No."

"So Gus figured—with Ike Potter's help—that an accomplice stood guard while the bomber went down to the 800 level, then walked about three miles underground to D-shaft where he planted the bomb?"

"It appears that way."

"And you think Gus went out to the mine to check out this theory?

"Except I don't believe Gus actually intended to go underground," said Muirinn. "He just wouldn't have done that."

Jett sat back. "That's one helluva trek underground."

"Which means the bomber must have been in good physical shape, right?" she said, pushing a strand of damp hair back from the bandage on her forehead.

Jett caught the scent of her shampoo.

"Or very determined." He got up suddenly, walked to the windows. He stood with his back to her, hands thrust deep in his pockets as he stared out over the ocean.

"That part of Tolkin had also been shut down due to low yield at least four years prior to the blast," he said quietly, trying to imagine the scenario. "Only a guy who'd worked that part of the mine before it was shut would even begin to know where to go in those abandoned tunnels, alone."

"So you think the bomber was likely a veteran miner?"

He nodded, pursing his lips. "Plus, he was an explosives expert. At least that's what the FBI thought." Jett rubbed his brow, that unspecified sense of foreboding gnawing deeper into him.

Muirinn sighed heavily. "I wish we could find someone we can trust who knows more about tracking, Jett."

"What use would a tracking expert be? The boots that made those prints would've been thrown out years ago."

"Yes, but maybe an expert could tell us something more about the *men* who made those prints. You said yourself the tracks in the black mud looked odd, like the bomber was dragging his leg or something."

Nausea swirled in his stomach.

The thought that several people in this town were protecting a mass murderer galled him. "Whoever that bomber was—" he said quietly, watching the water "—he sure as hell trusted his accomplice."

"What veteran miners might have that kind of a bond, Jett?"

He could feel her watching him intensely. He was nervous about turning around, meeting her eyes again.

"Those kinds of bonds do develop in life-and-death professions, like mining." Jett said softly. "Think about it, Muirinn. Each day those men enter a cage that is dropped miles down straight into the earth. There's no day down there, no night. Just total darkness. And there's this awareness of the tons and tons of rock and gravity pressing down over your head, held back only by manmade tunnels." He exhaled, thinking of his dad, and what Adam Rutledge had been forced to endure each day of his working life—a life that had made him a cripple.

He turned slowly to face her. "Those men are faced daily with inevitable accidents, death."

She cast her eyes down, and Jett knew she was thinking of her own father.

"Some of them deal with this threat by becoming fatalists—they just put their life in God's hands each day and go down into that mine."

"Is that what your father did?"

"No." He shook his head. "My dad didn't believe in fate. He was what they call a perfectionist. He used to say Tolkin killed only foolish miners. He said it was smarts, not God, that would keep him alive. He learned to know that rock like he knew the backs of his own hands, Muirinn. He'd study it carefully, figure how to slant drill holes at just the precise angle, put in just the right amount of explosive—enough to shatter it apart without disturbing the drifts where men worked, or endangering lives."

"So Adam was an explosives expert. Plus, he'd have known that closed-off part of the mine?"

"What are you saying?"

"Nothing. I was just wondering how many explosives experts worked Tolkin at the time of the blast."

"A lot," he said crisply. "Look, I don't like your insinuation here. My father—

"I'm not saying Adam had anything to do with murders, Jett!" she interjected. "I'm just saying that your father would know those veteran explosives experts, and I was thinking that maybe he could *help* us."

Jett's chest tightened, his thoughts turning grudgingly to the odd bootprints in the black mud. "If my dad knew anything, Muirinn, anything at all, he would've told the cops a long time ago."

"And they could have buried it, just like they buried those crime scene photos that Ike gave to Gus and erased the prints."

He held her gaze, his body growing cold.

"You were explaining about the bonds that develop between miners, Jett," she urged softly.

He didn't like where she was going with this. He didn't like anything about this line of questioning. "The perfectionists were also the best producers," he said coolly. "Which meant they earned the largest bonuses, sometimes even coming out financially ahead of the mine managers. As a result—and because they knew how to stay alive—that young and ambitious miners often tried to latch onto a perfectionist—to work under him, to learn the craft. Those bonds are legendary in the industry."

"Who latched onto your dad, Jett?"

Silence hung between them for several beats. "Where are you going with this, Muirinn?"

"Nowhere. I'm just interested."

He studied her a long while. "Chalky Moran."

Her eyes widened. "A *Moran?*"

He gathered up their empty soup bowls and carried them to the kitchen.

Muirinn came up behind him, not daring to get too close. "Chalky is the younger brother of the police chief, Don, right? The one you said married to the mayor?"

"Yeah." He rinsed the bowls, not looking at her.

"What is Chalky Moran doing now?"

He snorted, gave a wry smile as he stacked the bowls in the drying rack. "Chalky went into real estate when he left the mine. The Lonsdale family owns a good percentage of the buildings in town."

She hesitated. "Is he still tight with your dad?"

He slapped the dish cloth down abruptly. "Yeah. They still go fishing and hunting together." His eyes crackled with tension.

"Jett—" She almost reached out to touch him. But he visibly flinched and stepped past her, making for his booze cabinet. He poured himself a whiskey, then held up the bottle to her. "I take it you're not drinking at the moment?"

She shook her head.

"Can I get you anything else?"

"No, thank you."

He stalked out onto the deck, clearly needing space.

Muirinn felt guilty for being here at all. She sank wearily back onto the sofa, and closed her eyes.

She'd angered Jett by talking about Adam. She hadn't meant to. Muirinn was merely curious as to what kind of bond might motivate someone to keep the heinous secret of mass murder, and perhaps even kill for it twenty years later.

The image of Adam Rutldege hobbling out of that yellow bus in his Draegers sifted up from Muirinn's subconscious, and her thoughts turned again to the odd prints in the black mud...

No, it wasn't possible.

Besides, someone with Adam's disability was not likely to be able to negotiate a seventy-story climb both ways, plus hike a total of six miles underground. She'd seen herself just how crippled Adam had been on the day of the blast—it was burned indelibly into her memory.

Adam was a rescuer, not a killer.

Jett came inside to refill his glass.

Muirinn was nestled into the sofa cushions sound asleep, breaths coming soft and light, her eyelids fluttering with some private dream. Her hand rested on her rounded tummy.

He set his glass down, fetched a soft blanket and draped it carefully over her, tucking the corners in.

Then he sat and watched her sleep as the hours ticked by. The sky turned indigo, then deep purple as the midnight sun hovered just below the horizon.

Her hair had dried into soft springy ringlets, the auburn color rich against her pale skin. Her lips were parted slightly as she breathed. Unabashedly, Jett allowed his gaze to trace the curve of her breasts, her swollen belly. Lust grew hot inside him, hardening his groin with a sweet aching need.

He lurched to his feet suddenly, tension torquing too tight for comfort. He poured another shot of scotch, went back outside.

It was almost midnight now.

An eerie green summer aurora borealis pulsed across the sky, and the scent off the ocean was fresh. He leaned against the railing, watching a ghostly cruise ship move silently over the water. He sipped his whiskey.

Warmth spread through his chest, the taste of peat smoke, silky, smooth. Gus had bought him the bottle to celebrate Troy's tenth birthday. Jett missed the old man. He owed him.

Without his help, Jett would have lost his son.

Gus had never spoken to Jett about Troy's start in life, not after that initial phone call when he'd alerted Jett to the fact that Muirinn was giving their baby up for adoption.

During that call, Gus had told Jett that no matter what Jett chose to do about his son, Gus was never going to talk to Muirinn about it or interfere in any way. That was between Jett and her, but Gus had wanted him to know that Muirinn was giving away his child.

Jett suspected that Gus had been hoping he'd contact Muirinn, and that they'd work out their issues and become a family.

Instead, he'd gone to Vegas, secured custody behind Muirinn's back, and then married Kim. For reasons that had seemed so right at the time.

Jett started suddenly as he sensed Muirinn coming up behind him. She leaned against the railing beside him, careful not to get too close.

He ached to reach out, touch her.

"It's so beautiful," she whispered, staring at the silent, billowing curtains of northern lights, a reverence in her voice. "I didn't realize how much I missed this view."

Jett closed his eyes for a moment, her scent, the sound of her voice, tumbling his mind into a confusion between then and now. He slanted his gaze to her.

Her red hair was a wild mass of curls, her skin like porcelain in this haunting light. Again past shimmered between present, and she looked all of nineteen again. And he felt all of twenty-two. And just as desperate for her. For all the wrong reasons.

He took a deep slug of his whiskey. "Maybe you should consider leaving Safe Harbor for a while, Muirinn. Until this is sorted out."

She stiffened. "Why?"

"Because then you'll be safe. Your daughter will be safe." He slugged the rest of the whiskey back hard, relishing the burn.

And so will I.

She gripped the balustrade with both hands, staring out over the ocean, features tight. "I hear what you're saying, Jett," she said crisply. "And I did think about that. But I refuse to allow someone who murdered my father, and my mother by default, to kill my grandfather and to now scare me and my daughter out of our own home."

He tensed.

"You're really going to stay in Safe Harbor? Long term?"

"Damn right I'm going to stay."

His pulse quickened.

He had to tell her. He couldn't keep this secret any longer.

But by the same token, she hadn't told him yet that she'd borne his son. She was keeping her own secrets. She might never tell him. What would that mean for them, if she couldn't be honest?

Jett could not go forward without complete honesty and openness. Not this time.

"I owe it to Gus, Jett, to finish what he started, to find the answers. How *could* I leave now?"

"Just as easily as you did the first time."

Her mouth opened. She stared at him in shock.

He clenched his jaw, said nothing. Alcohol, adrenaline, lust, the memory of her kiss—all of it simmered in his blood. He needed barriers. Truth.

Pebbles clattered softly down at the shore with the incoming tide, and he felt her glaring at him.

"Look, I'm sorry," he said. "I just think it might be best if you left town for a while."

"For your sake, Jett? Or for mine?"

"For all our sakes," he said crisply. "I don't think it's a good idea for you to be here."

"Believe me," she whispered almost inaudibly. "I don't want to be here in your house right now, either. This was your idea, not mine. And tomorrow morning I'm going home. I'm going to do this on my own."

"And what are you going to do at home, alone? Sit there with a loaded shotgun in case your attacker comes back?"

"It's better than sitting here." She spun around, stalked toward the open sliding doors. "Or you can get that friend of yours to watch over me!" she called over her shoulder.

"Gus should have gone to the feds with this right away— you know that!" he yelled after her. "He should've handed that evidence over the minute Ike Potter gave it to him! Before someone could steal it. I have no idea why he didn't."

She turned inside the doorway. "Maybe, Jett, he had his reasons. Personal ones."

"So personal he ended up dead?"

"Maybe he wanted to be sure of something before he went around accusing people and screwing up lives."

Jett laughed harshly. "Yeah, wouldn't want to screw up any more lives now, would we, Muirinn?"

She turned her back on him and went inside, slamming the door behind her.

Chapter 10

Muirinn awakened at the sound of a sharp rap and the bedroom door opening. She blinked, momentarily disoriented before realizing that she was in Jett's house, that it was Saturday morning. Shafts of gold sunlight angled through the blinds, and Jett stood in the doorway, hand on the doorknob, a fresh white T-shirt molded to his torso.

His jeans were faded, seductively low slung, his hair damp from a shower. Those cobalt eyes lasered into her, and the set of his jaw was defensive.

He wasn't handsome, thought Muirinn as she sat up, reflexively bunching the sheet up over her chest. To her mind, handsome meant pretty, and this man did not qualify. There was nothing gentle about his physique at all. Jett looked rough, rugged—like the wilderness he'd grown up in, the place that defined him. The place he loved.

Something stirred in Muirinn's heart, an insistent voice that told her she needed to follow through on her threat last night and get the hell out of this man's hair, pronto, before they both got hurt again.

"Breakfast's almost ready." His gaze tracked over her as he spoke, and she saw his fist tighten on the door handle, cording muscles along his arm.

"Good morning to you, too," Muirinn said, reaching for her robe. His eyes followed her hand, a dark lust shifting into his features. Muirinn sensed his anger, too, rolling off him in quiet waves. After eleven years of silence, she'd invaded his space, his house.

His marriage.

And she felt awful. But the hot, sexual, intensity in his eyes invaded her body and, in spite of herself, warmth surged through her belly.

He grunted, closing the door softly.

Muirinn blew out a breath of air, tossed back the covers and pulled on her robe. Cinching the belt around her nonexistent waist, her attention was drawn to a framed photo of Troy on the dresser. She picked up the frame and, in privacy, carefully studied Jett's son. Pain twisted deeper, uncorking memories of giving birth to a baby boy, of how it had torn her apart to hand him over—feelings she'd managed to lock down in a part of her mind.

Feelings now being stirred back to life by Jett.

She wondered where their child was now, who he'd become. A wave of anguish and fresh guilt crashed through her, stealing her breath.

Muirinn set the photo down, inhaling shakily. Would their son perhaps try to find his real mother and father someday? Would he hate her for having abandoned him?

Would he ever understand?

Would Jett? If she told him?

Perhaps there truly were some secrets better left buried.

Or did that just lead to more tangled webs, more ruined lives, as Jett had so brutally reminded her last night.

Muirinn found Jett frying eggs and bacon in the kitchen, and the scent made her realize that she was starving.

He glanced up, and her heart squeezed again at the sight of him.

"Can you grab some napkins?" he said, jerking his chin toward a cupboard near the bookshelf. "They're in that drawer through there."

Muirinn moved into the open-plan living room, and reached for the drawer, but stilled as the cover of a familiar magazine spine on the bookshelf caught her eye. A copy of *Wild Spaces,* the high-end travel magazine for which she wrote. Her pulse quickened.

She glanced toward the kitchen, but Jett had his back turned, busy at the stove.

Muirinn quickly pulled the magazine off the shelf, flipping it open to where the corner of a page had been folded over. Shock rippled through her as she registered that Jett had book-marked a feature *she* had written.

Again, she shot a glance toward the kitchen. Jett had disappeared around the corner.

Muirinn quickly replaced the magazine, knocking a book over as she did. And stacked behind that book she found every issue of *Wild Spaces* from the past year, along with a DVD of a television show that had filmed Muirinn on assignment in the Sahara, where she'd been working on a story about the Dogon tribe in the Homburi Mountains near Timbuktu.

Muirinn's heart began to race—he'd kept in touch by following her career. While he'd told her that he never wanted to see or hear from her again, he'd been reading her stories, watching her on TV.

She hurriedly flipped open the cover of another magazine. This one had a corner turned down marking the page that contained her own bio; *Muirinn O'Donnell grew up in a remote coastal town in the Alaskan wilderness....*

Her vision blurred.

He still cared. Always had. But while he'd been keeping tabs on her life, she'd been doing everything to isolate herself from his.

"Want coffee with—" He froze, plates in his hand, as he saw what she was looking at.

Silence thrummed between them.

He turned abruptly, set the plates on the dining table with a clunk, stalked back into the kitchen and returned with the coffeepot.

He set it down heavily, motioned for her to take a seat, taking one himself. The look on his face was thunderous, his body tense, a dark and powerful undertow humming through him.

"You *subscribed* to them?"

"Sit, Muirinn," he replied coolly. "Your breakfast's getting cold."

She came right up to him, standing above him, the magazine in her hand. "Why, Jett?" she whispered. "Why have you got my magazines?"

The muscle at the base of his jaw began to pulse, a small vein swelling on his temple. "Muirinn—"

She wagged the magazine at him. "How'd you know I wrote for them?"

He said nothing. The wind outside soughed through the pines. His chest rose and fell heavily, his fist tightening around his fork. He was bottled rocket fuel, ready to blow. And she wanted him to blow.

"Talk to me, Jett!"

He dumped his fork onto the table, anger smoking into his eyes, his glare so direct and intense her cheeks flushed hot.

He lurched to his feet. "Get dressed when you're done eating," he said crisply, gathering up his plate, still full of food. "I need to do some work on one of my boats."

"Now?"

"Yeah, now."

She grabbed his wrist. "Don't—" she said, glowering at him. "Do not walk away from this."

He stilled, vibrating under her touch, his features like cold granite. He was so close she could smell soap, the warmth of his skin, the fresh scent of laundry.

"So it's okay for *you* to walk?" he said darkly. "To just up and leave Safe Harbor, to never look back? But not for me?"

"How did you know where I worked, Jett?" she said quietly, still gripping his wrist.

"Gus told me."

Anxiety edged into her. She glanced at the photo of Kim and Troy, thinking of her own baby. "He told you what?"

Jett held her eyes for a long, loaded beat. "Muirinn—"

"Tell me!" Her voice went higher and she hated it. "How did you know where I was?"

Did Gus tell you about my baby?

He glanced down at her hand gripping his wrist. Embarrassed, she let him go. He stepped back from her, and sighed heavily as he raked his hand through his hair. "Gus said that after California you went to Nevada."

Nerves tightened, memories of giving birth, the adoption in Vegas. Her eyes began to burn, her pulse to race, the tension of not telling him squeezing her chest, wanting to burst out. Fear stopping her from allowing it to.

"Did he say anything else? About Nevada?"

He held her eyes for a long, loaded beat, and she felt as if he knew something. "Should he have, Muirinn?" he asked very quietly.

She swallowed, her hand going automatically to her tummy. His eyes followed the movement to her belly. "He said that after Nevada you went to London for two years, and then to New York, where you got the job with *Wild Spaces*. I subscribed to the magazine."

"Why, Jett?"

"Because I was interested!" he snapped. "Wouldn't you be? Oh, wait. Why would *you* be interested—you who didn't bother to come home once in eleven years to visit your own grandfather. Or me."

Her cheeks flushed hotter. "Why in hell would I visit *you*, Jett? You went and got married! You who wouldn't deign to come with *me* to California. But you went off and got married in Las Vegas!" In spite of her best efforts, tears pricked hot into her eyes. "And then I *couldn't* come home, could I? Because you couldn't be there for me anymore."

He went stone still.

"That's the reason?" he said, very quietly.

"The only reason."

He paled. The muscle at his jaw pulsed and his eyes sparked. It made them fierce blue.

"What did you think, Jett?" she said, emotion balling painfully in her throat. "That I could come home to watch you with a new wife, and a new… " her voice hitched on the thought. "A new baby when, when I had just…"

Given ours away.

But the words wouldn't come.

She just couldn't tell him about his son—not right now, maybe not ever. She cast her eyes down. "The news of your marriage nearly killed me, Jett," she whispered hoarsely. "It's the reason I never came home, and it's the reason I need to get out of your house now, because…"

"Muirinn—"

She looked up slowly, swallowed at the rawness she saw in his eyes.

"I'm not married, Muirinn."

Speechless, she stared.

"What…what do you mean?"

"Kim and I separated six years ago," he said quietly. "We've been officially divorced for five."

Her skin felt hot, then ice-cold as the sea breeze wafted through the open window, blowing strands of hair across her face. The stitches Dr. Callaghan gave her yesterday began to throb on her temple. "But I saw you," she whispered. "With Kim down at the dock."

He cleared his throat, a range of emotions twisting his features. "Kim and I have an amicable relationship, Muirinn. She's great with Troy. She offered to take him to camp." He tilted his head slightly toward his drafting table. "I'm working on a large project, and I was going to use the time while Troy was away to finish it, draw up proposals for more funding."

Muirinn drew in a shuddering breath, and reached for the back of the chair, her mouth dry.

Her entire world had just been turned on its head and was spinning wildly. Suddenly, everything seemed possible, wide open, no bearings. "So…you and Kim share custody?"

Something flickered through his eyes. "No," he said softly. "I have custody of Troy. It's complicated."

She couldn't speak.

She just stood there staring at him, reality fading into the sound of wind in the pines, the crunch of waves down in the bay.

How many times had she looked into those cobalt eyes, heard those same sounds when they were in the shed by the water? They seemed to be melting past into present, the lost years crumbling to dust at her feet, and Muirinn was suddenly disoriented.

He took a step closer to her. Gently, he removed the magazine clutched in her hand, and set it on the table.

Muirinn's heart began to race.

He reached up, touched the side of her neck, his palm warm against her cheek. She shivered.

"I used to watch that video, Muirinn," he whispered roughly. "I'd look at your face, your smile for the camera…" His fingers closed around the back of her neck. "No matter what I said all those years ago, I couldn't *stop* caring about you."

He slid his warm hand slowly down her neck, and along her shoulder, slipping it under her robe, exploring the curve of her shoulder, the feel of her skin. He lowered his head, breathing her scent in deeply on a shuddering breath, his mouth so close to hers.

Heat arrowed to her belly, and her world spun, everything whirling into a wild blur around her and Jett, as if they stood at the heavy and silent eye of a kaleidoscopic storm.

"And I never stopped wanting you back," he whispered, blue eyes devouring her, his body trembling with hunger.

"It was impossible to go down to the ocean, to see that shed on Gus's beach and not remember that last night."

The night we made our son.

She swallowed.

The night we fought so bitterly and parted with such stubborn anger in our hearts.

Her eyelids fluttered as he slid his palm down the length of her arm, causing her robe to fall back off her shoulder. She was vaguely conscious of the wind increasing outside, the faint tinkling of chimes down at the boat shed.

"That night…you told me you hated me, Jett." Muirinn's voice came out thick. "You were so angry—you said you'd never speak to me again if I left."

"Would you have come back if I hadn't said those things?"

"Yes," she whispered, tears forming in her eyes, rolling down her cheeks. "God, yes. I would have come back, I would have come home to you."

His mouth twisted as he fought to control something inside himself.

"I've made mistakes, Jett," she said quietly. "Terrible mistakes. And I wanted to come back. I wanted to call you, to talk to you, to tell you that… "

That I was pregnant with our child.

He waited, willing her to finish, his eyes lancing hers, his entire body vibrating at some dangerous, elemental level.

But her voice cracked. "…then I heard you'd married and it was too late."

He closed his eyes for a moment, tempering the raw volcanic power of his own emotion. He moved his hand lower down her arm, encircling her wrist like a large cuff. "Did you love me?" he whispered roughly.

"Always." The word came out on a breath, soft. Urgent.

He drew her closer, so close her swollen belly pushed hard up against his pelvis. Her vision blurred as she felt his arousal.

She reached for his hand, placed it on her abdomen. He splayed his fingers, exploring the rounded shape of her tummy, and the shudder of a sigh escaped his chest. Closing his eyes, he slowly moved his hand to her waist, then up to her breast.

Muirinn's breathing became shallow as he rubbed his thumb over her nipple. His lips opened slightly, lust swilling black into his eyes as he felt her nipple harden under his finger.

And Muirinn couldn't focus on anything other than the pure sensation of his touch. To finally feel his hands on her body—to feel him wanting her, to know he always had—went beyond words, beyond her wildest dreams. Beyond all logical thought.

Shaking against his control, Jett drew her even closer, and Muirinn slid her hand up the back of his neck and guided his mouth down to hers. A groan escaped Jett as his lips met hers.

And something inside him snapped. He yanked her tight against him, thrusting his fingers up into the thick hair at the nape of her neck, as he crushed his mouth down hard onto hers.

Hunger blinded Muirinn as she felt him forcing her lips open, his tongue tangling, warm, salty with hers. He slid his hand up her thigh, under her robe, cupping her buttocks under her nightgown as he pulled her even tighter against his hard, hot body. Against the length of his erection.

An exhilarating wild heat coursed through Muirinn as this man who'd fought so hard to control his feelings for her finally lost it in her arms, moving faster. She hooked her leg around him, as he cupped her buttocks, lifting her up into himself as he kissed her deeper. Muirinn placed her hand between his thighs, relishing the rigidity of his erection under the rough denim of his jeans, oblivious to anything but the desperate, sweet, aching urge to have him inside her, all of him, as close to him as she could possibly get. She began to fumble urgently with his zipper.

He pulled back suddenly, eyelids heavy. "Muirinn—" his voice was hoarse, intense. "Are you sure?"

"Yes," she whispered. "I've never been more sure of anything."

Chapter 11

Jett eased Muirinn back onto the mattress of his double bed. She was naked, hair spreading out in a fiery halo of curls over his pillows.

Soft summer sun filtered through the floor-to-ceiling windows in his bedroom, warming his bare skin as he stood over her, staring down at her with tenderness and wonderment in his heart. He couldn't believe that she was actually here, in his bed, *all his,* beautiful in the glow of her pregnancy. And the lost years between them seemed to melt into a liquid sensation that knew no time.

Jett needed to take her hard, hot, fast—he needed to possess her—but he was afraid. He didn't want to hurt her.

And he wanted this to last.

She smiled up at him, lowering her lids as she studied his naked body unabashedly, drinking in every inch of him. His arousal grew hotter, heavier between his thighs as her scrutiny lingered there.

Lust shifted her features, glazing her eyes. She sat up, reaching out for his hands, the movement parting her legs, deepening her cleavage. Jett's mouth went bone dry as she took his hands, drew him closer.

She rolled a condom onto him, her movements smooth, tortuous, teasing, along the length of his erection. Jett's eyes rolled back and his vision swam with swirls of scarlet and black as she coaxed him with rhythmic strokes. He wasn't going to be able to make this last.

Quickly, he got to his knees, and gently placing a hand on each knee, he parted her thighs.

Muirinn felt his tongue, lips, and a silent cry swelled in her chest. Pregnancy had changed things in her. Everything felt fuller, more swollen, nerve endings heightened to excruciating sensitivity. She began to shake almost instantly as his tongue entered her, pressure, blood, building low inside her.

And she shattered, gasping between breaths and rolling contractions.

His control snapped. He flipped her quickly onto her side and, spooning his body against her back, he entered her from behind. The penetration in this position was shallow, but still she gasped as her body accommodated his size.

He moved, slowly at first, then faster, harder, hotter.

Muirinn clamped her hands down on the mattress, nails digging deep into the sheets as she came again, exquisite rolling waves of contractions seizing hold of her body. But she wanted more, the orgasms just seeming to increase her need, not satisfying something deeper. Because even in his hunger, Jett was being careful, not going deep enough.

Breathless, her skin now slick with perspiration, she swung

around, and pushed him onto his back. Holding his wrists above his head, she straddled him, and eased slowly down onto him, controlling the depth of penetration herself.

Muirinn threw her head back, and closed her eyes, savoring the sensation of Jett inside her.

She began to rock her pelvis against his, feeling the swell of her tummy rub against the rough hair low on his abdomen. He clamped his hands suddenly on her hips, guiding her. Faster, urgent.

Bracing her hands on his shoulders, hair tumbling forward over her face, he rocked her faster, harder. She grew breathless, dizzy.

The wind outside increased, branches tapping on the windows.

His fingers suddenly dug hard into her hips, and he stilled. She looked down into his eyes, and he bucked up in one hard thrust, releasing. And she came again, this time powerful, blinding.

She sank down onto him in a pile of loose, jellylike limbs. And she saw that he had tears in his eyes.

Muirinn gently kissed away a salty drop as it tried to escape down a tanned crease at the corner of one eye. He smiled at her— so open, so warm, as if all barriers between them had crumbled.

But they hadn't.

Because the pressure to tell him about the baby she'd given away had just mounted intensely inside her, but the prospect of his reaction was now even more daunting.

This thing between them was so precious, so gossamer fragile, she was absolutely terrified to shatter it right now.

And that fear of losing it all again made her feel especially vulnerable.

But he wrapped himself protectively around her, nose

nuzzling into her hair, breathing in her scent, and they lay like that, listening to the branches tick on against the window. "Sounds like another storm coming," he murmured against her neck.

"Doesn't matter," she said softly. "I feel safe here."

Jett grinned, but inside he felt suddenly edgy.

Never had he been so fulfilled by the act of sex, but neither had he been left so empty, needing so much more. Because he wanted it all now.

He wanted Muirinn to stay with him and Troy, for them to finally be the family they were always supposed to be. But he had to do this right. He had to find a way to carefully broach the subject of Troy, and the thought daunted him.

The last thing he wanted was a major confrontation with Muirinn. The last time they'd fought it had cost them both. Dearly.

Because he could see now just how much she'd suffered, too.

But the longer he hid the truth from Muirinn, the worse it was going to be.

He closed his eyes, thinking, imagining how it could all still go so wrong.

The wind was picking up outside, beginning to buffet the branches of a pine against the deck railing. Jett got up, wrapping a towel around his waist. He stood at the windows.

Whitecaps were flecking the inlet, and he wondered if he should bring his boat on shore. He reached for the binoculars he kept on the dresser, and scanned the water and mountains in the distance. It looked like bad weather ahead, judging by a dense band of cloud beyond the peaks.

"What are you doing?" Muirinn said from the bed, her voice husky, warm.

"Just looking."

"For bad guys?"

He laughed, his chest expanding with affection, warmth. He glanced back at her.

Muirinn's fire-gold hair tumbled in a mass of tangled curls over creamy white shoulders and breasts, and her cheeks were flushed, eyes glowing. He couldn't let her go again. Not ever.

He turned back to the window, tension whispering inside him, a movement from Gus's house next door suddenly catching his eye. Jett panned his scopes over to the property next door. "Lydia Wilkie's on your deck again," he said, adjusting the focus.

Muirinn sighed. "She's *always* in that house." She got out of bed, wrapping the sheet around herself, and came to stand by his side. "I guess my grandfather liked the company."

"Does she bother you?"

"Maybe. No. I don't know." Muirinn hesitated. "I was going to tell her that I didn't want her housekeeping services. Then again, once the baby comes…" her voice trailed off.

Jett's hands tightened around the scopes. "Are you really going to stay?" He made sure there was no emotion, no inflection in the question.

She bumped him playfully. "How could I not, after that."

He grinned. "I'm serious."

Her smile sobered. "My roots are here, Jett. I don't have any family left, but this is where I feel a sense of belonging more than anywhere else. I had to leave to learn this, and I want my daughter to feel that same sense of identity."

He inhaled deeply, a fragile hope flaring like a burning coal inside him. So much could still go haywire. They needed time. They needed less pressure. But this case, Gus's files, Tolkin, their own secrets—it was all putting the delicate beginnings of this new relationship into a pressure cooker, with a timer set to blow.

He thought again about the prints in the dark mud, and it hit him suddenly. "You know, I have an idea. Do you remember Trapper Joe?"

She frowned, pulling the sheet higher over her breasts. "You mean that old hermit who used to live way out in the bush?"

"That's the one. He still lives in the bush, and if *anyone* can tell us anything at all about those prints, it's Trapper Joe."

"He's a nut job, Jett."

"Yes, but his tracking ability is also borderline psychic, Muirinn. Last year he helped our SAR crew track down a missing twelve-year-old boy who got separated from his family on a hunting trip. For three weeks we found no sign of him at all. Everyone had given up. Even the family. And then one night old Trapper Joe shows up like a shadow out of the forest, and he just walks into the woods, and starts tracking. He found that kid in two days. Alive."

"Maybe Joe had something to do with the kid going missing in the first place. I wouldn't put anything past him. He always reminded me of an old stray wolf preying around the outskirts of town, looking to steal anything anyone left out."

Jett shook his head. "I've seen what he can do, Muirinn. Sometimes he comes into town, goes to the outfitters store on Main Street. He doesn't talk to anyone, but he watches them. He studies the way people move, the way they dress, what shoes they wear. I'd swear he can identify the prints of just about everyone in Safe Harbor."

"Okay, so he found a kid, and you're sold, but—"

"He was also at Gus's funeral, Muirinn. I think helping us will mean something to him."

She went dead still, color leaching from her face. "Why didn't you tell me he was at the service?" she whispered.

"You didn't ask. I saw Joe at the back of the church

during the ceremony. When I looked again, he was gone, like a ghost."

"Why?" she asked softly. "Why do you think Trapper Joe came to the funeral?"

"Because Gus was one of the few villagers Joe actually did communicate with. I saw him at Gus's house a couple of times over the years. I figured they were friends, in some weird way. Well, as much as Joe could be a friend to anyone."

"Where's Joe now?"

"He runs a trapline up north, has a camp out there."

"Maybe we should go see him, Jett. Even if Joe can't tell us anything about those prints, I'd like to know why he really came to the funeral. Maybe Gus spoke to him about his suspicions."

Jett nodded. "I'll fly us in, as soon as you're dressed." He tilted his head toward the window. "We should go before that weather behind the peaks rolls in. It'll also give us an opportunity to check out those ATV tracks from the air. Besides—" Jett wavered suddenly, then smiled. "There's something else I want to show you."

"What?" Eyes so clear and green and open looked into his.

"You'll see."

A smile ghosted her lips. "A secret?"

"No," he said quietly. "I'm tired of secrets, Muirinn."

She swallowed, forcing a smile that never quite reached into her eyes, nodded and left the room.

And Jett's whispering unease intensified.

Perspiration beaded the woman's lip. She swiped it away angrily with the base of her thumb. "What part about making it look like an accident did you not understand?"

"It was supposed to seem like a *hunting accident*—"

"Shooting up an entire shed, blowing up a truck?" She swore at him.

He jabbed his finger at her. "Do not swear at me. I am not a goddamn *murderer.* The woman is pregnant. Besides, we've got the laptop and photographs—"

"She's seen them!"

"So? She won't be able to prove a damn thing without them."

"But she can *talk.* And the fact that she hasn't reported the theft of the laptop, *or* the shootout at the mine, tells me she doesn't trust the cops. And that in turn tells me she's read the old man's files."

Panic shot across the man's features. "Do you think she's told Rutledge?"

"Of course she has." She inhaled shakily, pressing her hand against her sternum. "We've *got* to do something. This can't get out. We cannot be exposed."

"What do you propose we do, then?"

Her eyes darted, bright, manic. "The only thing we *can* do. We nip this in the bud. Now. We take them *both* out of the picture."

The man shook his head. "For God's sake, no. I can't do this. I am not a killer."

"Oh yes you are," she said. "Twelve men died in that mine because of *you*—"

"But I didn't—"

She held up her hand. "It doesn't matter. If this gets out, you *will* spend the rest of your life in prison."

She gripped his shoulders with both hands, perspiration shining on her forehead. "Think ahead. Think clearly. Think of the future." She paused, her mind racing. "It'll be easier to go after her alone, first. We find a way to abduct her, quietly. We take her out to the cabin, alive. And we use her to lure

Rutledge out into the bush. Then we make them both vanish."
She clicked her fingers near his ear. "Into the wild, a trip into
the bush gone wrong. It happens often enough."

Nausea roiled in his stomach.

He couldn't look at her, be with her. He went to the
bathroom instead, and threw up.

Leaning on the basin, he stared into the mirror, no longer
recognizing the man who stared back at him. He swore,
swiped his hand hard across the back of his mouth.

Twenty years had passed. And it still wasn't over.

Chapter 12

As they drove to the airstrip, Muirinn asked suddenly, "How come you were the one to get custody of Troy, Jett?"

His heart skipped a beat, but he kept his eyes focused on the road ahead. "Kim was okay with it."

Muirinn waited, but he volunteered nothing more. She turned in the car seat, back to him, staring out the window, and he sensed the shift in her mood. They'd just shared a deeply personal experience, and here he was holding back. Again. His hands tensed on the wheel.

As they neared the turnoff she spoke again, not looking at him. "What actually happened between you and Kim? Why didn't things work out?"

"You happened."

She shot him a glance. "I don't understand."

He heaved out a sigh. "Kim knew that I'd never gotten over you, Muirinn. She knew she'd always walk in your shadow, and she just got so darn tired of trying to *be* you, to take your place in my heart."

And she knows you'll always be my son's mother. Your eyes look back at her every time she looks into Troy's.

"Separating was for the best."

Silence filled the cab of the truck.

"Did she love you, Jett?"

Guilt gnawed at him. He'd tried so hard to trick himself into forgetting about Muirinn, to love Kim fully. He moistened his lips, nodded. "Yes, very much. She's a good person, Muirinn. A good...mother. And I loved her back, in my way. But Kim's happier now. She has a new man. It was the right thing to let her go."

"What does she do?"

"Nurse."

"Like your mom?"

He nodded. "Yeah. She gets on real well with my mom, and my dad, too."

Her hands fidgeted in her lap, restless. He neared the gates to the airstrip.

"Do you ever think that some secrets really are better left buried?" she asked softly as they drove through the gates.

That subtle sense of foreboding rippled through him again. "Why?" He pulled up alongside one of the hangars, where his plane was parked.

"Because maybe the truth is worse."

"What makes you say that?" He removed his shotgun and ammunition from the gun box, then opened the passenger door, holding his hand out to her.

She didn't take it right away. Instead, she looked directly up into his eyes. "What if we know the killer, Jett?"

He studied her for a moment, conscious of the growing

sound of a single-engine prop coming in for a landing. The airstrip wind sock was stiff, pollen blowing on dry, warm wind.

"I'm sure we will know him, Muirinn," he said, frowning. "It's a small town, and someone's been living here among us, keeping this old secret for a long time."

She clasped his hand, and he helped her out. She stilled in his arms for a moment, and Jett's chest ached. Damn, he loved her. Even more, if that was possible. Yet, oddly, he could feel her slipping from his grasp even as he held on. "Muirinn, what's worrying you?"

She inhaled deeply, a strange emotion crossing her features. She pulled away and rubbed her face, suddenly angry, conflicted by something. "It's nothing. I'm fine."

That icicle of unease that had crystallized inside him earlier burrowed a little deeper. He handed her the shotgun. "That's my plane over there," he nodded toward a stubby de Havilland Beaver parked in the hangar. "I'll be right back—just going to check in with the guys, tell them where we're headed."

She took the gun from him, unable to meet his gaze. Jett was really worried now. She was hiding something from him, and it was eating at her. Anxiety snaked through him. If she suddenly confessed to him that she'd given up his son for adoption, he was going to have to explain what he'd done— how he'd gone after Troy behind her back, how he'd raised her boy without ever telling her.

It wasn't going to be pretty. She was going to be hurt, furious. She might never forgive him.

He stalked over to the Safe Harbor Air offices, a sense of things closing in and pressing down on him with the low pressure cell and changing weather.

Muirinn slowly turned around inside the hangar, taking it all in.

A dusty tarp covered something large in the far corner.

She walked over to it, her eyes adjusting to the light. Propping the shotgun against the wall, she lifted up a corner of the tarpaulin. Underneath was the fuselage of a small plane, partially built, without wings. Curious, she peeled the cover back some more. Dust motes floated up into the dim shafts of light.

She recognized the shape of the fuselage from the little models her father used to have hanging from the ceiling of his old workshop—the planes he used to dream of flying up in the sky as he went down into the earth each day to toil in the blackness of the mine. A lump formed in her throat at the irony, and Jett's words filtered into her mind.

"If Troy hadn't introduced me to model airplanes, to the idea of flying, I might have become a miner, not a pilot. He was the one who told me, when I was ten years old, that I could do something better with my life than go down that mine."

At least her dad had passed on his love of planes to Jett and, in doing so, something of him still lived on. But whoever had been building this plane seemed have stopped some time ago. The fuselage was thick with dust. Muirinn yanked the tarp back fully, coughing as she did. She froze as saw the name that had been tentatively stenciled on the side.

Muirinn of the Wind.

Her heart caught in her throat. With trembling fingers, she reached up, smoothed off the thick layer of dust.

As she did, a shadow behind her blocked the light.

She swung around, heart thumping. She'd clean forgotten the gun, everything.

Jett stood silhouetted in the entrance, posture rigid. "What are you doing?"

He came up to her, reached for the tarp and jerked it back across the fuselage, covering the name, as if to hide a corpse, something offensive that shouldn't be exposed to the light of day, to human eyes.

"It's a Tiger Moth, isn't it?" she said softly. "Like the models my dad had, like the ones in Gus's photos from the war." A sudden rush of memories squeezed to her chest as she spoke.

Muirinn could almost smell her mother's baking again, hear the sound of teaspoons chinking against china, the patter of rain against the window. She could see Jett—her young neighbor on whom she had the biggest crush—building model airplanes with her dad as her mom served tea and cookies.

"De Havilland Tiger Moth, a replica," he said, watching her eyes. "I was building it when you left. It was going to be a surprise."

"You never finished her. Why?"

His eyes darkened. "Because you left."

She swallowed hard.

"We should go, Muirinn. This weather will bring rain by tomorrow, if not sooner."

"You named her for me," she whispered. *"Muirinn of the Wind."*

He said nothing.

She reached up, touched his face, her heart aching. "I love you, Jett," she whispered. "God, I love you."

He took her in his arms suddenly—hard, fierce—and he kissed her mouth. She melted into him, kissing him back, her world swirling away in a blur of time.

Someone coughed loudly. "Hey, you two lovebirds!"

Jett stiffened, and shock rippled through Muirinn. She pulled back. Adam Rutledge stood at the entrance to the hangar, hands stuffed into pockets of his coveralls as he grinned broadly.

"Adam!"

"Dad?" Jett said. "I didn't know you'd be here today."

Adam came forward, his smile broadening in his tanned, lined face as he held his hands out to Muirinn. "I heard you were back. Welcome home, Muirinn!" He clasped her shoulders firmly. "You're looking fine, girl. Wow, all these years. It's real good to see you." He shot his son a quick glance, not managing to hide a flicker of concern.

Jett scowled subtly, warning his dad to shut up, not to mention the kiss. Or the pregnancy.

He didn't. Instead, Adam stepped back, slapped his son affectionately on his shoulder. "The guys in the office told me you were here. I came to see where you were headed."

"I'm taking Muirinn up for a spin before that weather over the ridge rolls in."

He nodded, eyes thoughtful as Jett declined to elaborate. Adam stuffed his hands back into his coverall pockets, turned to Muirinn and smiled warmly. "Well, I hope Jett's going to bring you around for Sunday lunch tomorrow, Muirinn. The missus likes to cook up something special for the weekends." He cast another quick look at his son. "Too bad Troy won't be here."

Jett smiled, but the light didn't quite reach his eyes. "Yes."

"So, you coming tomorrow?"

"Wouldn't want to miss Mom's cooking."

"See you both Sunday, then." Adam hesitated, something unreadable creeping into his eyes, a worry, perhaps, that his son was going to get hurt again by this woman. "Fly safe," was all he said.

Jett nodded.

Muirinn watched as Adam hobbled toward the hangar entrance. His injuries and arthritis had worsened over the years, and he was dragging his left leg with each awkward swing of his gait. While still strong and solid, mining had clearly taken its toll on Adam Rutledge's body, thought Muirinn. She wondered if he was in constant pain. Jett followed her eyes, a frown crossing his features. "Come," he took her elbow, turning her away from watching his dad. "Time to fly. You got those photos with you?"

She nodded, looking back over her shoulder, eyes still trained on Adam as he crossed the grass outside the hangar.

"Muirinn?"

She shook herself. "Sorry," she said softly. "I just can't help wondering what it might be like to have my parents around, too." Her eyes were soft. Sad.

"Hey," he tilted her chin up. "We're going to do right by your parents, Muirinn. We're going to get to the bottom of this, and we're going to find justice. Someone will pay."

She bit her lip and nodded.

Before flying out to Trapper Joe's, Jett flew northeast of town, guiding his barrel-chested plane between the avalanche-scoured peaks that surged up either side of the Tolkin Valley. The plane's characteristic growling made headsets necessary to talk without yelling.

Through the blur of the spinning prop, Muirinn recognized the old headframes of Tolkin Mine coming into view ahead. She shuddered involuntarily at the memory of being under fire in that dank shed.

Jett dropped altitude, banking his craft tightly along the flank of the mountain, then suddenly he pointed. "Down there!" The mouthpiece gave his voice a tinny quality. "See them? ATV tracks, along that dry portion of narrow mountain trail." He dipped his wings sharply, and followed the tracks, the de Havilland's belly almost skimming the tips of the trees.

The trail below them crossed a dry creek bed, then disappeared into forest. Lifting the nose sharply into the blue sky, he banked and flew low over the tracks again.

"Are you sure those are the sniper's tracks?"

"I saw dust kick up when the shooter fled. The only thing you can drive up those trails is either a four-wheeler or a dirt bike. And look, the tire marks lead straight from his hide above the Tolkin Mine site to the trail there."

Anxiety unfurled inside Muirinn. "And where does the trail itself lead?"

"Up through the saddle in the mountains over there—" he pointed. "And then back down into the drainage on the other side of this ridge. You can go all the way along that eastern river drainage back to Safe Harbor, approaching the town from the other side."

"So the shooter could have come from town?"

"Or from one of a handful of remote hunting or logging camps up the next valley."

Jett pointed the nose of his craft northward and, as the foothills faded behind them, the horizon grew flat and endless. Below them a herd of caribou fanned out in a thunderous race across the plain, spooked by the buzz from his prop.

"Down there," Jett said suddenly as he buzzed low over the forest again, just skimming the treetops.

Below them, miles of aquamarine lake shimmered between white shores and dense forest. He pointed to a small log cabin in a clearing cut along the north end of the lake. "That's what I've been working on. A high-end, rustic fishing lodge that will attract clients from places like New York and Texas. There's also a big market for this kind of thing in Germany and the Scandinavian countries."

He dipped his wing sharply left, swooping over the

clearing. "The main lodge will go over there." He pointed. "With satellite cabins along the shore there." He pulled up the nose of the Beaver and flew west, the rugged craft rattling and growling. "You can see how that tributary from the Tuklit River feeds in at the head of the lake over there. Perfect for salmon fishing."

Muirinn peered down through the side window as Jett banked the plane for her. A massive grizzly appeared, lumbering along the shallows of a pebbled spit.

He grinned as he caught sight of it. "Brown bear, wolves, caribou, moose—it's God's country, Muirinn."

She turned to look at him. "Those blueprints in your house—they were for this place?"

He grinned again, a wicked slash of white against tanned skin, his mirrored glasses glinting under his helmet. She'd never seen him like this, in his plane, in his element. Pure, happy, all-male.

And Muirinn realized with a start that they had always, at the core, been exactly the same.

While she'd seen those granite peaks as a rock prison, so had he. Only he'd been able to escape, up here, with wings. And because of it, he'd found freedom. To leave and return whenever he wanted, on his own terms.

While she'd left and hurt the people she'd loved the most.

Jett tilted the de Havilland's nose upwards, and they climbed again before leveling out over a wide valley of muskeg. A male moose with full set of antlers jerked his head up at the sound of the plane, and took flight through tussock as they buzzed over him.

Muirinn felt her heart soar as the vista took hold of her soul. Almost subconsciously, she placed her hand on Jett's thigh. "This is gorgeous," she whispered.

"I wish I could have brought you up eleven years ago, Muirinn."

She glanced at him, unable to read his eyes behind the mirrored shades, but she knew what he was saying. Maybe if she'd found this freedom with him, instead of looking for it away from him, they'd still be together.

A family.

Because if she'd stayed, she'd have kept their son.

Muirinn's mood shifted as her thoughts turned to the adoption. *How would you feel about me if I told you about our baby?*

He shot her a concerned glance. "What's up?

"Nothing." She forced a smile. "I was just thinking how good it is to see you happy, Jett."

And how I'd hate to do anything to destroy that.

They flew farther north in silence, the vast beauty brooking no conversation. Or perhaps it was a looming sense of foreboding as the sky grew darker, more oppressive.

Jett took the plane down alongside a sullen river. He landed on a gravel bar, wheels bumping wildly over the spit next to the wide and silent body of water. His prop slowed as they came to a halt near a crude wooden rack hung with strips of drying salmon flesh.

A deathly silence seemed to descend over the plane, broken only by the pop of hot engine metal, and the sharp *krak* of a raven perched high on a dead snag.

A cloud of midges hovered over discarded salmon guts at the water's edge. Two scarred dogs were eating the scraps. They growled, heads low, then scuttled into the brush as Jett climbed down from the pilot's seat.

The air felt sticky, close.

He helped Muirinn down from the plane, suddenly keenly

aware of his hunting knife at his hip. And as they crunched over a small stone beach, Trapper Joe appeared, his grizzled form silently separating from the dense shadows of the trees, shotgun in his hand. He watched them approach, lowering his weapon only when he recognized Jett. He pushed his cap back on his head, nodded his greeting.

A silent man.

A secretive man.

A man like so many before him who had fled north, escaping something—perhaps the law, or a dark secret—hoping to hide from the past in this vast and isolated wilderness, under the cover of the long, dark winters. It was out here that men like Joe hoped to start another life. But invariably that didn't happen. Because the problems came with them. And Trapper Joe's problems, his secrets from south of the 49th parallel, were hidden behind bloodshot eyes, too much whiskey, sun-baked and wind-worn skin. And silence.

He was a man of indeterminate age who lived completely off grid. A survivalist, with only his dogs for company.

No one knew his story, where exactly he came from. Local lore pinned him as an escaped con from Down South. The kids Muirinn grew up with used to say he had murdered a man. Adults, however, pegged him for an ex-cop. One who'd gotten on the wrong side of his badge. They cited Trapper Joe's almost paranoid avoidance of local law enforcement as proof.

But regardless of Trapper Joe's secret, those who knew of his ability to track found his art almost mystical.

"Joe—" Jett nodded, showing the old trapper the bottle of whiskey he'd brought with him, not wasting words on a man who didn't like to use them. "We were hoping to show you something, ask your opinion."

Joe narrowed his eyes onto Muirinn.

"This is Muirinn O'Donnell, Gus O'Donnell's grand-daughter."

Trapper Joe said nothing, just turned and led Muirinn and Jett through the trees to the clearing where his camp had been set up.

Mosquitoes buzzed in a small cloud. Two Husky-Malamute crosses got up, growled. Joe waved them away, and they retreated a few feet to lie silently, watching, like barely tamed wolves. Again, Jett reminded himself that his knife was handy. Joe ducked under a tarpaulin that served as a deck cover and led them into the log cabin, motioning to a camp chair and sawed-off log for seats. Jett placed the bottle of whiskey on the Formica table.

The interior smelled of wood smoke and the cloying scent of wet dog fur. Strung along one wall were an assortment of animal traps and a pair of old gut snowshoes. Joe went to his woodstove, poured coffee, black. "Got no cream," he said, plunking the chipped mugs onto the table.

He sloshed a dollop of whiskey into his own, offered the bottle to Jett and Muirinn. Both declined with a shake of the head.

Joe took a seat, his eyes still fixated on Muirinn. It made her feel uncomfortable. Jett tried to break the ice. "You haven't seen Muirinn for a long time, huh?"

"Gus said you were a looker. He was right."

Muirinn flushed. "Thank you."

"You weren't at his funeral." Joe's voice was creaky, as if from disuse, but it didn't disguise the accusation in his words.

Guilt washed through her. "I was stuck out in a jungle, in Irian Jaya, the Indonesian half of New Guinea." She found herself trying to justify her absence again. "It's one of the last places on earth where there are still tribes that have had no contact with the rest of the world, and no one could get news to me," she said, *needing* Joe to understand. "It was part of the project, to feel as cut off from communication as the locals of the area."

He sipped his coffee, eyes unwavering. "Even though you was pregnant?"

Muirinn felt her cheeks warm again. "I was entering my sixth month. My doctor said everything was good. Plus, our photographer was a qualified paramedic." Muirinn cleared her throat, feeling small, judged. "Gus must have really meant something to you, Joe, for you to have trekked all the way into town for the service," she said.

He studied her in silence. "What do you want me to look at?"

"These." She slid the four photos onto the table.

He pursed his lips, gray whiskers standing out. He tapped his dirty fingers on two photos. "These two were taken down inside the Tolkin Mine."

Muirinn glanced at Jett, heart pattering. They'd been hoping to avoid too many specifics. But she couldn't lie now—not if she wanted his trust. "Yes. How do you know?"

Joe picked up one photo, his thatch brows lowering as he examined it more closely. Then his eyes shifted up slowly, warily, and met hers. "What you want to know?"

"Is there anything at all that you can tell us about who might have made those prints?"

"Why?" he said quietly.

Muirinn exhaled cautiously. She'd hoped it would be easier. But Joe had read enough already to make Muirinn believe that if she were less than honest, he'd clam up. She needed his trust. "Gus was trying to solve a mystery."

"The bombing."

She nodded.

Jett leaned forward. "Joe, the reason we came out here to see you was—"

"Was because you don't want anyone in town to see these," he cut in, shaking his head. "Gus spent years trying to solve this thing."

"Did he ever discuss it with you?"

The trapper didn't respond. He just stared at the photos.

"Joe," Muirinn said, leaning forward, "my grandfather believed that the bomber had an accomplice, and that means there are at least two people who might still be out there trying cover up the murder twenty years later." Muirinn paused. "These photos recently came into Gus's possession, and those prints could belong to the men responsible for killing my father. And, yes, right now it's best that no one knows that Gus had these. It could be…dangerous."

"You think it was what got Gus killed?"

"What makes you think he was killed?" Jett asked, very quietly.

"No way Gus went all the way down that shaft alone. No truck. Nothing. It didn't smell right to me." Joe wavered, as if weighing the potential blowback for what he was about to reveal next. He cleared his throat. "Two people were at the mine with Gus the day he died."

Muirinn's pulse quickened. Jett placed his hand on hers, warning her to go slow with Joe.

She swallowed. "What makes you say that?" she said, voice cracking.

"Prints. I saw them at the scene. Left by a man and a woman." A nerve began to twitch under his eye. "They were with Gus. And they killed him."

Chapter 13

Muirinn's heart thudded. But suspicion unfurled slowly through her. "How do you know this, Joe?" she asked very quietly. "Were you there?"

He moistened his lips, lifted his cap and scratched his head. "I went to look after I heard they'd brought up his body. That's when I saw the tracks. They told me Gus was not alone when he died."

"But how could you tell?" Muirinn asked. "There must have been police and rescue personnel tracks all over the place—"

"My own prints included," interjected Jett.

His gaze shifted to Jett. "The SAR people's boots have individual identifying marks in the heel lugs, right?"

"That's right," said Jett. "It was something we started after that kid and his family went missing in the bush. We did it so that trackers like yourself wouldn't confuse our prints with the prints of the missing."

"So that trace from you and your team could be excluded right off. Cops issue boots, too. I know who wears what shoes. You get a good mantracker, he can tell a whole story—like finding a fossil. You can build the whole damn dinosaur. You can see who came first, who walked on top afterwards, what the weather was like."

Again, Muirinn was reminded of the old rumor that Joe was ex–law enforcement, or ex–military. It fit. It was why Jett had thought Joe might actually be able to help them.

But what he was saying raised more questions.

"Why did you go to the mine after they'd brought my grandfather up, Joe? Was it because you didn't buy what the police were saying about his accident?"

He shrugged, avoiding eye contact suddenly. "I liked Gus," he said, as if that explained it all. The fact was Joe found very few reasons to like any humans at all. If he was admitting a fondness for her grandfather, it probably meant a hell of a lot.

"And you didn't think to mention this discovery of yours to the Safe Harbor police?" Jett said.

He cast a withering look at Jett. "I mind my own business. They can mind theirs."

"Tell me about the prints, Joe. What led you to believe my grandfather was murdered?" Muirinn swallowed the sharp lump swelling in her throat as she spoke. Jett reached out, covered her hands, and she realized they were clenched tightly in her lap.

Joe drained his coffee, swiped the back of his hand hard across his mouth and splashed a few fingers of straight whiskey into his mug. "This is how I read it. Gus was on the Tolkin property, and he was looking for something. He had a flashlight with him—"

Muirinn threw Jett a questioning look.

Jett nodded. "He did. A flashlight was found with his body."

"So that tells me Gus went there to poke around somewhere dark, maybe look down a shaft. His prints were going back and forth between the Sodwana headframe and D-shaft."

"Like he might be timing how long it would take between the two points underground?" Muirinn offered.

Joe nodded. "Yep. Like that. But he's not feeling well, okay, or maybe he's tired, or he's thinking and pondering, or confused, because he shuffles some, sits down a couple of times."

"As if he might have been short of breath, or his heart was giving him trouble?"

"Yep. That would do it. Then tracks from two people intersect with his, and they stop and talk to him. You can see this from the prints."

Joe's whiskey-coffee breath was strong, and Muirinn felt slightly queasy. She glanced out the door, suddenly craving clean air. Suddenly afraid of what Joe was going to say.

"You okay, Muirinn?" Jett said softly, hand on her shoulder.

She nodded, mouth dry.

"What can you tell us about those two sets of prints that intersected with Gus's tracks?" Jett said, taking over for her.

"One set was made by a man, hiking boots, size 12. Other set was probably from a woman. 'Bout a size 6."

"A woman? You're sure?" said Jett.

"Well, could be a young male, but the prints looked like a woman's running shoes to me, and the gait was more like a female. So my take is that this couple comes up to Gus, they stand and they talk. Then they start walking with Gus back to Sodwana. Then they stop and there's a tussle. And from that point on, the prints change. Woman is walking on one side, man on the other. Gus in the middle. Tight formation. The couple's gait is sort of angled in toward Gus, like they was pushing him, escorting him. And then Gus's stride, the depth of depression changes, like he is reluctant, leaning back, maybe collapsing, dragging his feet a bit."

Muirinn swallowed, nausea deepening.

"By this time, they're getting close to the headframe building, and their trace gets all messed up with all the other prints that came later. Police-dog prints all over them, too."

Silence.

Heat intensified in the cabin as the sun baked down outside.

A mosquito whined near Muirinn's head, and one of the huskies whimpered softly, paws twitching in his dream as he slept near the door.

Jett broke the gravitas.

"Why does that scenario say murder to you, Joe?"

"Because it tells me Gus was forced to the headframe building, and then I figure he was forced down into the shaft by those two people, because, like I say, Gus wouldn't have gone down there alone." He shrugged again. "Maybe once down there on the 300 level, in the dark and heat, the stress of it all gave him the heart attack. Thing is—those two people never told anyone he was down there. That's murder in my book."

Muirinn tensed, perspiration prickling over her lip. "What else could you tell, Joe?"

"The prints went back to D-shaft, just the two sets, no Gus this time. And they went to where two vehicles were parked behind the main D-Shaft buildings. The woman got into one vehicle, and the man into the other. Both vehicles had standard truck tires, one with winter tread and a real heavy oil leak. Left a black puddle."

Muirinn chilled. An oil leak. Winter tires.

Gus's vehicle?

Maybe he *had* driven out to the mine, and one of those

people had driven his truck back to his house to hide the fact that Gus was ever at the mine.

She glanced at Jett. He hadn't touched his coffee. Neither had she.

A soft wind began to swoosh through the stunted conifers outside, a pine cone clunking onto the metal roof.

Jett cleared his throat. "Joe, Gus's housekeeper said he was gone three days before he was actually reported missing. Then it took another thirteen days before we found his body down the shaft. And you're saying you could read all this information from prints that were made on the day of his death? Because those prints would have been over two weeks old."

Joe's eyes narrowed. "The time lapse is what helps tell me the story. Who was there first, who came after. There was rain the night before Gus went out to Tolkin. His prints, and the prints from the man and woman, were made in wet mine silt. Then they baked solid under hot sun for the next couple of weeks. That gray glacier silt bakes good as damn clay. Easy to see what prints were made atop of those."

Muirinn thought of the fine gray silt Jett had pointed out when he'd come around to fix Gus's truck. It could have come from the shoes of one of the two people who'd forced Gus down the mine shaft, after they'd driven Gus's truck back to his home to cover their tracks. "How come the police or SAR didn't look for any of this?" Muirinn snapped suddenly.

"It wasn't being treated as a crime scene, Muirinn," Jett said quietly. "To be honest, we were all just looking for an old and eccentric man who'd wandered off."

Muirinn's mood darkened. "And how do you know those two photos were taken down inside Tolkin Mine?" She pointed angrily to the crime scene shots Joe said were taken underground.

"Mud down there is very black, especially at the deeper levels. Anyone can see this was shot in a tunnel."

"And what can you tell us about those underground prints?" Muirinn's voice came out thick.

Trapper Joe studied them for a long moment. He got up, opened a drawer and retrieved a big old-fashioned magnifying glass. He pored over one of the photos in silence. Muirinn swatted at a small cloud of bugs, the smells in the cabin growing more cloying as the sun rose and the heat baked down.

"See there—" Joe pointed with a blackened fingernail. "And there—the smoothness in the lugs of the sole on the one side? This man favors his right leg. His left is injured, and from this wear on the sole, it's a permanent disability."

An unspecified chill stole into Jett, despite the heat in the cabin.

Joe held their eyes for a moment, running his tongue over his teeth, waiting. But neither Muirinn nor Jett offered him more information.

He grunted, turning his attention to the next photo. "From the ruler alongside this underground print, *these* tracks were made by a size 10 winter work boot, Vibram sole, standard mining issue. You can still buy these from Big Bear, the Safe Harbor outfitter on Main. This trace was made by a well-built man, solid, judging by the depths of the boot depressions, maybe 'bout five-eleven if we're looking at an average ratio between foot length to height. His limp is pretty bad—it would be real obvious to anyone watching him walk." Joe creaked his chair back, got up and began to imitate the limp, conjuring up the man's movement from the prints. One long stride, a swing of the left hip, then a short stride accompanied with a drag of the leg. "And he was getting tired. Like this." Joe dragged his left leg more.

The chill deepened in Jett as he watched Joe, an image of another man filling his mind, a man who made the exact same movements Trapper Joe was making.

A man both he and Muirinn had just watched hobbling out of the airport hangar.

He felt Muirinn glance at him, but Jett did not meet her eyes. He stared instead at the table, telling himself it was nonsense—lots of men working Tolkin had these kinds of injuries, not just his father. It was an occupational hazard.

And five-eleven was a pretty damn average height.

Joe piled the photos neatly, and pushed them abruptly back toward Muirinn. "If I was a betting man," he said looking at Jett very intensely, then Muirinn, booze and the scent of stale sweat wafting across the table as he moved, "I'd say the owner of those boots worked the mine. 'Cause—" he watched Jett again "—if this man went down to the 800 level at Sodwana and hiked all the way underground to the blast site, he'd have to know where he was going. He'd have worked that section before it was shut down, known those tunnels and rock like the backs of his own hands. And he'd have to know his explosives." He rubbed his stubbled jaw. "You ask me, you're looking for an experienced miner who was blasting rock in that old section before it closed. To be that experienced, I reckon he wouldn't have been younger than thirty at the time of the blast. Add four years from when the Sodwana section was closed, then another twenty years since the blast—your bomber is older than fifty-four. Could even be in his sixties now."

Jett felt the blood drain from his face, but he said nothing. Again, he told himself that tons of miners could fit that profile.

What if we know the killer, Jett? Maybe some secrets really are better left buried.

He felt sick.

Joe was watching him oddly. Heat and claustrophobia closed in on him. He needed to get out of this place.

Jett lurched to his feet and stomped out of the cabin.

Muirinn and Joe followed him. "Jett?" Muirinn said, placing her hand on his arm, but he shrugged her off and kept walking. "That storm is going to be coming in soon. We need to leave."

The wind blew hotter and harder, a soft rushing sound beginning in the tops of the conifers as they walked in awkward, ominous silence back to the plane, Joe following behind, shotgun in hand.

As they took off, Joe stood watching them from the beach below, until he was just a tiny speck alongside the wide brown river in a vast and lonely wilderness.

Muirinn sat quietly, watching Jett. His hands were tense on the controls, a muscle at his jaw pulsing. She knew he had to be thinking of his father—how could he *not* be?

Because she sure was.

The image of Adam Rutledge hobbling out of the hangar was burned fresh into her brain, and Joe had mimicked Adam's movements so exactly it was almost as though he'd morphed into Adam himself for a ghostly split second.

"Do you trust him?" Muirinn said as the plane reached elevation and leveled out.

"Joe?" Jett exhaled heavily, features grim. "I trust him not to go to the cops, if that's what you mean."

"I mean, can you trust that he knows what he's talking about? About those prints, that man and woman. The two vehicles." She hesitated. "The limp."

"Joe might be short on words, but not brain cells. He's sharp. I told you what he did with that kid."

Muirinn peered down at the ground below as they flew.

"That could have been Gus's Dodge leaking oil at the mine, Jett," she said softly. "And there was gray silt in his cab. If those two people were walking in wet silt at the time, it would have caked to their boots, and it would explain how so much got into the bottom of Gus's truck."

He shot a sharp glance at her. "So you figure Gus drove his own truck to the mine, and either that man or woman drove it back?"

She closed her eyes, resting her hand on her tummy, tired suddenly. "I don't know what to think," she whispered.

Silence hung for several beats, broken only by the whine and rumble of the engine.

"I guess I'm scared of the truth, Jett, of what we might find," she said softly. "If it's all connected—the Morans, the police—the truth could blow this town and families apart again, just as if we'd planted bomb in Safe Harbor ourselves."

Jett said nothing, eyes focused dead ahead as he flew.

And Muirinn's mouth turned dry.

It wasn't just the town that would blow apart. If they found out that Adam did have something to do with the death of her father, the truth could shatter for good the fragile beginnings of their relationship.

Muirinn sneaked another look at Jett's rugged profile. She understood something crucial now—the lies that could bind, and divide. Because as much as she wanted justice for her father, for Gus, for her mother, she sure as hell didn't want to blow Jett's life out of the water, or her chances of a future with him.

Muirinn sat back in the seat, a sense of looming, unavoidable disaster ahead as they came in to land at the Safe Harbor airstrip.

"I'm going to fly you out," Jett said suddenly as the plane taxied to a stop on the grass.

"What?"

He helped her down from the plane. "I want you to pack your bags, and then I'm going to fly you to Anchorage, see if we can get you on standby to New York."

"*Why?*"

He led her back to his truck. "Because this is more serious than I thought, Muirinn. And it would be safer for you and your baby to go home until this is settled."

He yanked open the cab door, waited for her to get in. But she just stood and stared at him, dumbfounded. "Jett," she said, "I told you, I'm not going back to New York. I'm staying in Safe Harbor for good. This is my *home.*"

Jett swallowed, tension beginning to roll off him in hot dark waves. "Please, get in."

She climbed into his truck, her mind racing, and he slammed the passenger door closed.

He started the engine and drove her back to Mermaid's Cove in unnatural silence, his features gray. "Please, *talk* to me, Jett," she demanded. "What the hell is going on with you?"

"Nothing. I just want you and the baby to be safe."

Urgency bit into Muirinn as he ushered her into his house. And she couldn't take it anymore. She swung around to face him as they entered his house. "Jett—"

He waited, laser eyes burning into her.

"You don't want me in New York because it's safe," she said, feeling as if she were going to the gallows with her next words. "You want me way out of the way while you deal with this, because you think your *father* might be involved."

"Look, Muirinn, if you're thinking my dad had anything to do with that bombing just because he has a limp, you're way off base!" He tossed his flight jacket onto the sofa and thumped his shotgun onto the table. He was nervous. Edgy. He aimed his index finger at her, eyes glinting cold. "My father tried to *save* your dad, but the security and the cops wouldn't let him and his mine rescue crew in."

"Why wouldn't they let Adam in?" she urged softly.

He glared at her.

"Because he was a union stalwart, okay? I didn't understand that when I was twelve, but I learned later it was because Adam Rutledge was a shop steward, and he was vehemently anti–scab labor. That made him an enemy of Troy O'Donnell, and an enemy of all those other men who crossed the picket line daily to earn a dollar to support their families, and to stop the banks from foreclosing on their mortgages."

He vibrated with anger, eyes darkening at her accusations.

"There was a court injunction against Adam and the union executives, prohibiting them from being on Tolkin property, Jett. Remember that? And *that* is why they wouldn't let him in to allegedly save my father."

Jett lowered his voice dangerously. "That doesn't make him a *murderer,* Muirinn."

"So what size boots *does* he wear, Jett?"

Silence.

"How tall is he?"

Pulsing, darker silence.

"Jett, it does fit. Your father was an explosives expert. He worked that section of the mine before it was closed. And Chalky Moran had latched onto him—Adam was Chalky's mentor, you said so yourself. Chalky could have been the accomplice, Jett. You also said Moran blood runs thick in this town. Think about it—why would Ike Potter, a rookie cop at the time, sit on those photos? Because it must have been a Moran who took them. And a Moran was also police chief at the time. Bill Moran could have destroyed Ike's career. And after Ike had left it so long, he must have gotten scared, because he'd have been implicated in a conspiracy to cover up mass murder if he'd come forward at a later stage."

Jett paled, his skin tightening over his bones, his eyes growing dark and hollow. The clock in the kitchen ticked loudly, and Jett felt sick. All that old crap resurfacing from that dank hole in the earth.

Too many goddamn secrets.

Why had she come back anyway—just to dredge up all this old stuff again?

"Jett—" she reached to touch his arm, but he drew back sharply and shook his head. "Do not touch me, Muirinn."

Hurt arrowed through her eyes. "I'm sorry, Jett," she said softly. "I was just connecting the dots. The limp, the left leg injured—"

"No! No freaking way, Muirinn."

"There's one way to find out, Jett. You could at least speak to him."

He swore again. Muirinn was forcing his mind to go where it didn't want to go, where he *couldn't* allow it to go. So he fought back instead, lashing out at her because he needed to strike out at the very idea itself.

"My father wouldn't do it. He's just not a murderer."

"And what makes you so damn sure? Just how far might *you* go to protect *him*? As far as…" she paled suddenly as the implication hit her. She instinctively placed her hand over her belly. Jett's expression tightened.

"What were you going to say, Muirinn?"

She shook her head, looking ill.

"You were going to say as far as trying to kill Gus? To shoot at *you?*"

Her mouth opened in protest.

But he raised his hand. "Don't even *think* it, Muirinn. My dad is a savior, a *rescuer*—"

"Maybe your father is the reason Gus did not go straight to the FBI with Ike's photos, Jett. Have you considered that? Maybe he wanted to be sure. Maybe Gus didn't want to hurt you or your family. And his hesitation got him killed."

Jett watched her hand on her belly, tore his eyes away and fixed them on her face instead. "My father," he said very quietly, "could not have blown up the men he used to sit elbow to elbow with in the Miners Tavern—"

"He didn't drink with those men during the strike, did he? When things started to get bad, when the town was divided, I'll bet Adam started drinking down at the union hall, along with the other stalwarts."

"Dammit! He did not try to cover this up! It's inconceivable. My father would never, ever hurt Gus. Or you." He stalked to the window, paced, dragging his hands over his hair. "For God's sake, Muirinn, there is just no way in hell my dad would try to murder his own grandson's mother!" He stalled as he realized what had just come out of his mouth.

He swung around, staring at her.

Her mouth opened slowly, and her face went ghostly white.

Time stretched, her eyes growing into huge dark-green pools of shock, horror.

"What did you say?" Her words came out hoarse.

He inhaled deeply, then released a heavy shuddering breath. "I said, my father would not harm his own grandson's mother." He paused. "The mother of my son."

Chapter 14

Muirinn felt the blood rush from her head.

"I...I don't understand."

Desperation twisted into Jett's face, and Muirinn's gaze slid slowly over to the photo on the wall. She stared numbly at the image of a smiling Troy sitting on Jett's lap in the cockpit of his de Havilland Beaver.

"Troy?" It was a rough sound that came from low in her throat. A sound she didn't recognize as her own.

Jett said nothing, grief, angst, agony wrenching his powerful features. And Muirinn knew.

"How?" It was all that would come out.

"You gave him away."

"How did you *know?*" she whispered hoarsely.

"After you told Gus that you were having a baby and had agreed to a private adoption, he called and told me. He gave me the name of the lawyer the adoptive couple was using."

She swayed, catching the back of the sofa for balance, unable to speak, face muscles in a vise.

"I sold everything I could, Muirinn—my bike, my fishing gear, my boat—and I flew down to Nevada, and I fought for my son. I wasn't going to see my boy, my own flesh and blood go to another family—"

"But *how* did you do it? How did you get him?" The words were barely a whisper.

He inhaled deeply. "I told the lawyer that I was the real father, that my child was being given away without my consent, and that I would fight for my rights every goddamn step of the way. The lawyer informed the adoptive couple, and they decided not to contest me. They didn't want a child on those terms, Muirinn. And they released the baby into my care."

Her stomach turned to water.

"And Kim?"

"I'd met her just after you left town—she'd come up here for a nursing job. We started dating, and she offered to fly with me to Nevada to get my son. I was grateful for her help, Muirinn. I was a twenty-two-year old guy who knew zip about infants. But Kim did."

Emptiness, exclusion clawed at Muirinn's insides. She'd been so terribly desperate, so alone and hollow after giving up her child. Missing her baby so terribly much. Meanwhile, Jett and some young nurse had him, warm in their arms. Without her knowledge. Tears swam into her eyes, blinding her, and they rolled down her face. She didn't care.

Their son. Troy. Living here with his real dad in Safe Harbor all these years, right next door to her grandfather. The lost years, the lost potential, the sense of betrayal—it was too vast, too painful to comprehend.

"So my grandfather *knew* that Troy was my son, and living

here?" She couldn't quite grasp that Gus had not once, not ever, told her any of this.

"Yeah, Muirinn, he knew. Gus told me you were having our baby because he didn't want his grandchild being raised by some other family. He wanted to give me the tools to make my own choices, because he felt it was my right as a father. I think, Muirinn, that Gus truly believed I would contact you, talk some sense into you, bring you home and make things right. But I married Kim instead, while we were in Vegas. And when Gus found out, he let things be. He was just happy to be able to watch his grandson growing up next door, anonymously."

The sheer scope of the deception—of Gus's deception— was suddenly suffocating, drowning her.

"Why…why didn't Gus tell *me* you had our son?"

"Maybe he would have if you'd ever bothered to come back to Safe Harbor to visit." The bitterness in Jett's voice sliced into Muirinn like a knife. "Or maybe he didn't tell you because I ended up marrying Kim, and Gus didn't want to mess with my marriage for Troy's sake. Kim was a good mother, Muirinn. Maybe Gus didn't want to force you to return out of some misguided sense of obligation and break up our family. Hell knows. Gus was different. He did his best. He wanted the best for you, too. He knew how desperate you were to escape this place, to 'grow,' he called it. He just wanted you to be free."

"Why *did* you marry Kim?" she whispered, feeling utterly defeated. "So soon."

"She loved me. I loved her back in my own way. I never thought I'd ever love anyone again the way I loved you, Muirinn. And I really needed her help with Troy. It was her idea to get married in Vegas, to return to Safe Harbor as a family, and it seemed right at the time."

"And your parents?"

"They know. I told my mom and dad. How else was I going to explain the sudden appearance of a tiny baby in my life?"

Muirinn's grip on the back of the sofa tightened as she felt her legs beginning to buckle.

"What about everyone else in town?"

Jett's eyes pierced hers. "Safe Harbor has clearly been pretty damn good at keeping secrets and minding its own business. I personally never said anything to anyone, and no one ever asked anything about the baby, even if they did have their suspicions. Dr. Callaghan knew Troy wasn't Kim's child. But everyone treated her as his rightful mother."

"Oh, God." Muirinn moved around the sofa, and slumped weakly down onto it. She looked up through her tears. "What about Troy, what does *he* know?"

"He thinks Kim is his mother."

"You lied to me," she whispered, then lurched back to her feet. "You bloody hypocrite. *That's* why you have custody of him, and Kim doesn't! She isn't his *mother.*"

"Don't—" He pointed his index finger at her. "Do not go calling *me* a hypocrite. *You* hid Troy from me. You gave him away to strangers. You have no right to call *me* a liar."

"How could you not tell me, even after we made love!"

"I needed to be sure."

"Of what?"

"He's ten years old, Muirinn. If I tell him that Kim is not his mother, everything he has thought to be true in his life will have be reevaluated. I'm not ready to turn his entire world upside down only to have you walk out on us again."

"I told you I was going to stay!"

"Muirinn," he said quietly, his hands trembling. "I still don't know for sure that you mean it. God knows you felt nothing leaving before."

She stared at him. "What do you want from me, Jett? What more can I do to make you trust me?"

He came up to her, took her hands in his. "I wanted time, Muirinn. Time to be sure that I wasn't making a mistake in opening that door to talk to you about Troy." His eyes bored hotly into hers. "And maybe part of me deep down felt that you needed to come clean first, and tell me what was my *right* to know— that you'd borne my child and given him up for adoption."

"And *my* right?"

"What right? You chose to leave. You *chose* to give him away. You never tried to find him again."

"I wasn't allowed to! It was part of the adoption arrangement. What was I supposed to do, Jett, when I found out that our last night together made me pregnant? I had no choice. I was alone. I had nothing. You told me you hated my guts, and never wanted to see me again."

"I said those things out of blind fury because you were abandoning everything we had, Muirinn!"

Her mouth tightened, and with the sense of betrayal surged anger. "All these years I could have watched him grow," she said quietly, bitterly. "Stolen away because no one told me."

"You didn't come home. You never once looked back—"

"That doesn't mean I didn't regret having done what I did! Giving my baby away was the worst mistake of my life, and I have never stopped regretting it. If…" her voice hitched. "If I'd only known there was a way back, a way to set things right…"

His eyes glistened, emotion ripping at him, daring him to crumble and break.

She swore softly. "So it's okay for you to have secrets, but not me?"

"I didn't want to hurt Tr—"

"Do you *honestly* think I'd hurt Troy?" she snapped. "Do

you think I wouldn't move heaven and earth trying to do the right thing by my son? Do you think I purposefully set out to hurt you, or *anyone* else? If that's the case, then to hell with you, Jett. Because I never stopped loving you." Tears streamed fresh down her face as she pushed past him, stalked to the spare room, grabbed her bag and started shoving her things into it.

"What do you think you're doing?" he said from the doorway.

"Getting out of your hair. Once and for all."

He grabbed her arm as she marched past him. "Muirinn, wait. We need to talk about this—" but she shook him off with force. "Get your hands off me!"

He let her go, undeniable rawness shimmering in his eyes. Yet under all the pain, she could still see his love. And that made it hurt all the more. She felt like crawling into the abyss that had yawned open at her feet, and just curling up and dying.

She stormed into the living room and grabbed a shotgun and a box of shells from his gun rack.

"Muirinn—"

She slung her bag over her shoulder, flung open his front door and stormed out in the purple northern night.

"Muirinn, dammit, don't be so stubborn. Get back in here!"

She halted in the driveway, turning around. *"Stubborn?"* She raised her hand palm up, warning him not to move one step in her direction. "If you come after me, Jett, I *will* shoot you."

"It's not safe out there."

"And I'm safer with *you?* You've hidden my son from me for ten years, Jett." Her voice shook. "What else are you hiding? The fact that your father killed my family?"

"My father is not involved, Muirinn."

"Oh? Then you shouldn't have any trouble asking him about it. Or are you going to just ignore it, sweep that under the carpet, too?"

"You're doing it again, Muirinn! You're running away instead of facing things—facing me—working this out with me!"

"Oh, be a man, Jett, and face your own damn father before you can talk about facing me!"

She stomped off down the path and disappeared into the grove of woods between their properties.

Panic seared through Jett, followed by a crushing wave of sheer desperation. He knew Muirinn's temper—she *would* pull the trigger if he went after her now.

And he was worried about her baby, the stress he'd inadvertently put her under. Guilt beat at him. He still had to keep her safe, and he couldn't call the cops. This thing had spiraled way out of control, and he had no idea who might be involved.

So he called one man he did trust—his friend, Hamilton Brock, an ex-Marine who'd served in two Gulf wars. More than anything, Jett trusted Brock with his life. Brock also volunteered for Safe Harbor Search and Rescue and he'd put his life on the line for the team more than once.

As always, Brock was game to help Jett out, and said he'd be right over. Jett thanked him and hung up the phone, thinking about how his father had also regularly put his life on the line for men trapped in the mine.

Then you shouldn't have any trouble asking him about it. Or are you going to just ignore it, and sweep that under the carpet, too?

Muirinn was right. He had to talk to his father. Now. No matter what he discovered, he had to face this.

Jett waited in his truck at the top of Muirinn's driveway for Brock to arrive. He wound down his window and stuck out his elbow as he saw Brock's SUV approach.

"I left a message on her voice mail to say I was sending someone around. She didn't pick up, but I'm pretty sure she heard it. She should be expecting you."

Brock gave his twisted grin. "No problem." He hesitated. "You okay, bud?"

"Yeah. You just keep an eye on her, okay? I'll explain later."

Brock reached out his window, smacked his palm on the hood of Jett's truck. "No worries. She'll be waiting for you, safe and sound when you get back."

Jett drove to his parents' house. The northern night was dusky, but not dark. There was no moon, and an eerie stillness.

He slammed on the brakes suddenly as a coyote darted out from a bush and froze in his headlights.

Heart hammering, Jett waited for the animal to gather its wits and trot into the trees before putting the truck in gear.

But the incident had rattled him further.

What else are you hiding, Jett? The fact your father killed my family...you going to sweep that under the carpet, too?

The deep gut-honest truth was that Jett *had* thought briefly of his father when Muirinn first showed him Ike's photos, when she'd mentioned his dad's kinship with Chalky Moran. And Jett *had* brushed those thoughts right under his mental carpet. He didn't want to think it remotely possible that his dad might be the bomber, even though all the signs had been staring him in the face.

Could he have seen it years ago?

Had he subconsciously avoided facing the truth?

And how much better would that make him than the rest of the people who'd tried to bury the evidence—like Ike Potter or the cop who'd removed the photos?

Jett pulled his truck into his parents' driveway and sat for a moment, fighting his worst fears.

He *had* to ask his father outright. No matter what the consequences. Because he'd said it himself to Muirinn, the time for secrets was over.

Jett banged on the door.

His mother opened it, belting her robe around her waist.

"Jett? What is it? Goodness, you look awful. Come on in."

"I need to speak to Dad."

Worry flared in her eyes. "What's going on?"

Jett stepped past his mother and into the mudroom. He lifted up one of his father's work boots just as his dad came through the living room.

"Jett?"

He didn't reply. He turned the boot over, read the size on the Vibram sole. Size 10. His chest tightened.

He looked at his father.

Adam Rutledge stared at the boot in Jett's hands, then lifted his eyes slowly and met Jett's gaze. He said nothing, but Jett's heart sank at the expression on his father's face.

He put the boot down, marched into the living room, straight for the booze cabinet. "Want a drink, Dad? Because I sure as hell need one." He poured two fingers of scotch and downed the shot. Eyes burning, he poured another.

Jett's father limped into the room, cobalt eyes intent on his son. Jett watched his father's distinctive hobble. It was just as Trapper Joe had demonstrated—the perfectionist, an explosives expert, a veteran miner who bore the battle scars of Tolkin in his body.

And what scars did he bear deep in his soul? What secrets were buried there? What guilt?

"Where did you go in the plane today, son?" Adam said, jaw tight. "Who did you go see?"

"Trapper Joe. Gus had some crime scene photos of the bomber's prints down in the mine. Did you know that?"

His father swallowed. "No," he said quietly.

"We took those photos to Joe to see what he could tell us about the man who made them."

"Then you came here, to look at my boots?"

"Because the prints were made by a veteran miner with size 10 feet and a lame left leg—an explosives expert who had an accomplice waiting up at the Sodwana headframe while the bomb was planted."

Jett paused, giving his father a chance to offer some explanation. Some denial. But his father remained silent, neck muscles bunching, the fingers of his right hand twitching at his side.

"Did you do it dad? Did you 'fix' the strike by planting that bomb, killing twelve men?"

"Jett!" His mother admonished from the doorway.

"Stay out of this, Mom," he said coolly, eyes focused solely on his father, *willing* him to deny it, to offer some explanation, anything.

Instead, Adam Rutledge's face turned ash-white.

Nausea gushed up into Jett's throat, mixing with the acrid heat of whiskey. But he had to see this all the way through. He had to pick a side, and that side had to be justice. It was the *only* recourse, the only way to end the secrets, heal the rifts in this town.

It was also the only way to make things right with Muirinn.

He slugged back the last of the whiskey, slapped the glass down.

"Did you kill Gus O'Donnell, too?"

His father tensed visibly, saying nothing. Jett's mother started sobbing uncontrollably.

He turned to his mother. "Did *you* know that Dad rigged

that blast, Mom?" His voice remained ice cool. "Did you suspect what he'd done? Or did you just turn a blind eye that help bury it like the rest of this godforsaken town?"

Her sob turned into a wail, and Jett's heart plummeted even further.

He stared at his parents, eyes burning. "You're not going to deny *any* of this?" he said, unbelieving.

His mother just cried softly. His father glared, his body humming with tension.

Shaking with anger, Jett stormed out of the house, his entire world shattered.

The screen door slapped dully closed behind him, the sound echoing into the pale, moonless night.

Waves of violent anger, pain, regret all churned through him as he marched toward his truck.

The screen door suddenly swung open behind him, and Jett tensed, hearing his father hobbling out over the gravel.

"Jett!"

He couldn't face him.

Jett climbed into his truck, started the ignition and slammed the gearshift into reverse. He wanted to get the hell away from here. But he couldn't—he just could not hit that accelerator. His father had admitted nothing yet, and Jett still wanted desperately to believe that his dad was coming over to tell him it wasn't true, that there was some rational explanation for it all.

Staring dead ahead, fists tight on the wheel, he listened as his father's footfalls crunched over the gravel, coming nearer.

He turned slowly to look at him—the face he knew so well and had loved so deeply all his life. The face of a man he'd respected, the man who'd taught him so much.

His father clamped his hands down over the open window. "It was a mistake, son," he whispered hoarsely. "A *mistake*."

Jett felt sick.

He shut his eyes tight, gripping the wheel, his ears ringing as he fought the urge to punch down on the gas, flee from things he didn't want to hear.

His father's arthritic hands gripped the door tighter, gnarled knuckles white. "The blast wasn't supposed to kill those men, Jett," he whispered urgently. "They were not supposed to *die!*"

Chapter 15

The knowledge that his father was a murderer swilled dangerously inside Jett. "So you did do it," he whispered. "You're the killer."

"The blast was just going to be a warning, Jett, to spook management and scabs. We'd been without work for almost a year, and union funds were depleted. There was no more strike pay coming, and the longer those scabs kept working, the longer management could handle the strike, and the longer half the men in this town stayed unemployed. People were losing homes, they were being forced to leave town. The strike was killing this place—that mine was the only goddamn gig in town!"

"So you tried to fix it all with a *bomb?*"

"A warning! There were not supposed to be casualties, son." Adam's eyes glittered feverishly in the glow of the northern night. "The man-car carrying those men was not supposed to trigger the trip wire. The ore car—which is wider and has a third wheel that sticks out—that was supposed to trigger the explosion. But I was cold, wet. It was a long climb, a long hike underground, my fingers were numb from white hand. I... I must have gotten the trip line too close to the track. God knows, Jett, I have not lived a day without regretting what happened."

Jett couldn't even look at his father. "You killed Troy O'Donnell," he whispered. "You tore Muirinn's life apart."

"It wasn't supposed to happen, you've *got* to believe that!" Anguish torqued through his father's voice. He gripped the door tighter. "I did it for you, son. For your mother. We were desperate. If the mine stayed operational with scabs, it meant that men like me—the veteran miners who built this place— would go bankrupt. And if we couldn't buy stuff in the stores, the shops were going to go under, the support industries were going to go under, the whole damn town was going to go under. We would have lost our house, *everything*."

"You murdered people to keep the house I now live in," Jett said quietly. "I used to admire you, Dad." He shook his head. "I used to be so damn proud of you."

"I did it so we *could* remain proud. So I could care for all of you."

The irony hit Jett hard—the things people did for love, the secrets they hid, the lies that bound them, the ripple effect down through the generations. The lingering poison.

He thought of what he'd done to Muirinn, and she to him—for love.

"The deaths were a mistake." Adam whispered again. "But I never did *anything* to hurt Gus. Nor would I ever try to harm Muirinn. I am not a murderer, son."

Jett turned slowly to stare at his father. Tears glistened on the man's rugged cheeks. A man Jett had always looked up to. Admired. Now he could barely even look at him.

"Who was your accomplice? Chalky Moran?"

His father's mouth shut in a grim line. Silence hung for several beats. A coyote yipped somewhere on the outskirts of town, hunting neighborhood cats.

"It's in the past, Jett." Adam said almost inaudibly. "It's over. Can't we just leave it in the past?"

"It's *not* over." Jett ground the words out through clenched teeth. "Gus O'Donnell *died* because of those photos Ike Potter gave him. And Muirinn and her baby almost died, too, because someone out there is *still* prepared to kill to keep this secret."

"I swear on your mother's life that I had *nothing* to do with that," Adam said hoarsely.

"Then who did?"

"I don't know anything about that."

"Start with your accomplice. Was it Chalky?"

Silence.

So the identity of his accomplice was a secret his father still wanted to keep. A sick coldness slicked down inside Jett's belly. "Step back from the truck," he ordered quietly.

"What are you going to do?"

Jett didn't know what he was going to do with this mind-blowing news—that his father was the mass murderer who'd evaded an FBI manhunt.

He needed to think, process. Someplace where he could find distance, objectivity.

"What would *you* do, Dad?"

Silence.

"Step back from the truck," Jett repeated through clenched teeth.

And he drove off, leaving his father standing in a settling cloud of dust, his eyes burning with tears—the tears of betrayal.

Jett did not drive home. He headed instead for the unprotected cliffs to the west of Safe Harbor. It was a place that drew him in both good times and bad.

Easing his truck onto the grassy verge, he cut the engine. The night was clear, dusky, the sun not far below the horizon. But the peaks themselves were hidden by a dark band of storm clouds—the pending front was beginning to move in. He called Brock. "Everything okay there?"

"All quiet," Brock said. "Nothing going on apart from the old tenant awake, light on in her cottage down at the bay. Otherwise, nothing but raccoons."

Jett killed the call.

He stared out over the ocean, watching the timeless heave and pull of the dark water, listening to the soft crunch of waves at the base of the cliffs. And he tried to process the knowledge that his own father was responsible for a mass murder, a case that had been mothballed, never solved, the truth buried by people in this town that he'd loved so deeply.

A pod of killer whales, sleek as mercury, ribboned through the swells below, hunting seals as the midnight sun began to rise again over the distant peaks.

The world in beauty and death.

Beginnings and endings.

It was time for justice to be done, for the past to be put to rest. For new beginnings.

But to do that Jett would have to take his own father down. He rubbed his brow.

All he had to do was pick up the phone and call the FBI, tell them that his dad was a killer.

It wasn't as easy as one might think.

As the day brightened, Jett drove to the airstrip, picking up a bagel and coffee on the way. He wanted to get his plane into the air, get above it all during those rare dawn hours when the world was still pure. When he came back down to earth, he'd face his duty. He'd call the feds.

He parked his truck and headed on foot out onto the airfield, coffee in hand. Dew glistened on the grass, and on the wings of his plane as they caught the first warm rays of the sun.

After one more phone call to Brock, who said all was still calm at Mermaid's Cove, Jett swung himself up into his cockpit.

Muirinn watched dawn breaking over the sea, the loaded shotgun resting in her lap. All night she'd sat, absently rocking in her grandfather's bent-willow rocker, thinking about Troy.

Her son.

Another tremor of emotion ran through her body, and she placed her hand over her stomach.

Two children.

A son and a daughter.

Again her eyes filled with moisture. But with it came the anger, the profound sense of betrayal. And so it had been all night, waves of intoxicating exultation washing through her, alternating with shafts of bone-deep sadness at the sense of time lost with her son, exhausting her.

One thing Muirinn knew for sure was that as much as she might spark and simmer and clash with Jett, he was—and always would be—the father of her son. And she was not going to leave Safe Harbor.

She was going to give birth to her daughter here, raise her baby girl in this town, and watch her son grow into a man— from a distance if necessary.

She'd run the paper. Be a mother. Grow vegetables in the garden and show her daughter how to collect clams, just as Gus had shown her.

And God help anyone who tried to take that away from her now.

Because no matter how hurt Muirinn might be, Jett had done an incredibly bold thing going after his child, alone. It was the kind of move that defined him. He had a rock-solid core of values he was not prepared to compromise. And he valued family.

Then she thought of Adam Rutledge, and cold anxiety surged fresh through her. He was family, too. But she had to believe that Jett would do the right thing, and see justice done.

She had to believe in *him.*

Even if the rift between father and son meant she and Jett could never be together.

Finally, she slipped off, eyes closing as sleep claimed her.

Sun was hot on Muirinn's face when a noise in the hallway startled her awake.

Someone was inside the house.

She raised the shotgun, heart in her throat. "Who's there!"

"It's just me, Muirinn. Oh goodness, child, put that gun down. What on earth is going on?"

"Mrs. Wilkie?" Muirinn swallowed, disoriented. "I…it's nothing. I was having—" she laughed, embarrassed. "Just a bad dream."

The old woman frowned and tutted. "It's the baby. The hormones can do it to you. I've never had children myself," she said, setting her basket down on the kitchen counter. "But when my sister, Margaret, was pregnant with my godchild, she had vivid nightmares all the time. Chamomile tea really helped." She tapped her basket, smiling warmly. "I brought you some scones for breakfast, baked in my wood oven. And strawberries, fresh from Gus's garden."

She removed a cluster of smiling daisies from the basket, and busied herself emptying the older foxglove blooms from the copper vase and rearranging the daisies in their place.

Mrs. Wilkie had left the front door wide open to the bright morning, and a soft warmth drifted inside on the sea breeze. Muirinn glanced nervously at the door. She knew there was a bodyguard outside, yet she was suddenly filled with an unspecified sense of trepidation.

"I'll make you some chamomile tea, dear. It'll be good for those nerves, and for the baby." Mrs. Wilkie shuffled into the kitchen and took down one of the tea tins Gus kept on the shelf. "With a few sprigs of mint. You used to like that mix as a child, remember? I used to make it chilled for you in the summer."

Muirinn felt surreal, as if she couldn't believe the past events had actually happened, that she'd slept in a rocking chair with a shotgun. That this woman had just walked into her home with a basket of flowers and breakfast. Maybe she was just confused by the heat of the sun that had been on her face while she slept. Still, it seemed strange that Mrs. Wilkie hadn't really asked about the gun. Or mentioned the bodyguard outside.

"I…I'd love some tea. Thank you." Muirinn clicked the safety on her weapon, got to her feet, set the gun against the wall and stretched her back. Not only was she thirsty, she was starving.

Chimes tinkled in the breeze, and Muirinn glanced at the open door again. "Did you see anyone outside, Mrs. Wilkie?"

Mrs. Wilkie glanced up. "No, why?"

Muirinn frowned, wondering what had happened to the bodyguard Jett had sent over. Perhaps he was laying low, or maybe he'd left when the sun came up. Which was odd.

"Is everything all right, Muirinn, love?" Mrs. Wilkie asked, concern creasing her brow.

"I'm fine. Will you stay and join me for breakfast? I wouldn't mind the company."

"Of course I will, dear." Mrs. Wilkie reached for another china cup. "But no chamomile for me—" she grinned. "I need caffeine in my tea." She spooned a different herb mix into another small teapot, poured in boiling water and set both pots on the table with a little mat.

The tea was good, different from the way Muirinn remembered, but that might be because her mouth was so dry and fuzzy from adrenaline the night before. She sipped from her cup as she watched Mrs. Wilkie buttering scones, her bright gypsy skirt swirling around her ankles as she moved, her long gray hair caught back in a colorful scarf. It was comforting to watch her. Equally comforting was the soft, warm sensation that was beginning to flow outward through her chest, her body. With mild surprise, Muirinn realized that this tea was working fast—too fast. A faint dawning of fear whispered in her brain, but she couldn't quite harness the thought. Her mind was growing foggy. Then she heard voices outside the door—a man and woman.

She glanced at Mrs. Wilkie, her vision suddenly blurry.

Mrs. Wilkie was watching her intently, smile gone.

"Did…did you hear…that…" *Oh God, she couldn't talk, her tongue was thick and slow in her mouth.* Muirinn tried to lift her arm. It was heavy, as if she were trying to move through syrup.

Panic struck her heart, but she couldn't seem to react to it, to think straight.

"Mrs.…Wilkie…"

The woman said nothing.

Muirinn's brain swirled as she squinted at Mrs. Wilkie, the colors of her gypsy skirt morphing into a chromatic blur. The purple foxgloves lay on the counter behind her. So pretty. Pretty…as poison. It struck Muirinn suddenly— foxglove contained digitalis. The same medicine Gus had been taking.

Years ago Gus had told Muirinn that dried foxglove leaves could easily be confused with comfrey. He'd liked to drink comfrey for his health. But foxglove would stop your heart, he'd said.

Muirinn tried to look up into Mrs. Wilkie's eyes, to read what was going on. But her vision was too hazy, a halo seeming to shimmer around the woman's body. Mrs. Wilkie knew about herbs. She'd made Gus's tea blends.

She could have given him foxglove.

Mrs. Wilkie had also just mentioned her sister Margaret's pregnancy. Margaret was married to Old Man Henry Moran. And Margaret's child—Mrs. Wilkie's godchild—was Chalky Moran.

Jett's voice rumbled into Muirinn's fading consciousness. *Moran blood runs thick in this town…*

Mrs. Wilkie was protecting her godchild, her flesh and blood—and she'd put something into Muirinn's tea!

My baby… Muirin had get out of here, get help.

She tried to stand, bracing her weight on the table. But she slid slowly down to the floor as her legs buckled out from under her.

Mrs. Wilkie moved forward quickly.

Muirinn reached out her hand, trying to mouth the word *help*. But nothing came out.

Lydia Wilkie crouched down, stroking Muirinn's long, soft, red hair. "Sleep, child," she whispered softly. "You'll be with Gus soon. This town needs peace now. The past must sleep." Wilkie's eyes closed, tears spilling down her cheeks.

"Go in peace, my child," she whispered as Muirinn's world faded to black.

Chapter 16

Adam Rutledge had long dreaded the day his son might discover the truth about the Tolkin massacre.

But after twenty long, tortuous years of guilt and nightmares, Adam had dared hope that Jett might just be spared knowing what his father had done. But it wasn't to be. His nightmare had come true.

Not only that, but from what Jett had just told him, the toxic secrets from the mine were oozing up to rip lives apart all over again, and Adam could not—would not—let that happen.

He wheeled his Jeep into Chalky Moran and Kate Lonsdale's driveway, slamming on the brakes. Hobbling quickly up to the door, he banged loudly with the base of his fist.

No answer.

Adam went around back and saw that Chalky's big white van was gone. Peering in through the windows, he could see their gun cabinet hanging open. This felt wrong—way wrong.

As far as Adam knew, the only other people who knew what had really gone down on that cold spring morning twenty years ago were the Moran brothers, and now maybe Chalky's wife, Kate Lonsdale.

When the bomb had ended up killing those men, Chalky had turned in desperation to his brothers, and Don and Bill Moran had instantly rallied around their own, closing ranks to protect Chalky. Because of that, Adam had been spared, too.

Adam knew just how deep Moran blood ran, and just how much they all stood to lose if this got out, especially now that Kate was mayor. But just *how* far would they go to keep the old secret buried?

Could they have killed Gus?

He shuffled painfully back to his Jeep, the arthritis in his hip and knees acting up the more he moved. He called Jett on his cell phone, but the call went straight to voice mail.

Adam cursed. His son had disowned him, cut him off. He couldn't blame him, but he really needed to talk to him now.

Adam started his ignition and raced over to Mermaid's Cove. But Jett's driveway was empty, his truck gone.

Tension squeezing across his chest, Adam rushed over to the O'Donnell house, thinking maybe he'd find Jett there. But his son's vehicle was not in the O'Donnell driveway. Neither was Gus's red Dodge. The front door of the house, however, hung wide open.

Adam dragged his disabled leg up the stairs, pain worsening, making him break out in a sweat. He raised his fist to rap on the open door. But as he did, he caught sight of Lydia Wilkie hurriedly clearing dishes off the table. She glanced up, and at the sight of him in the doorway, a look of sheer horror—then panic—crossed her lined features. Her eyes were puffy, as if she'd been crying.

"Lydia?" he said, stepping into the hallway. "Is everything all right? Where's Muirinn?"

She seemed unable to speak for a moment, rooted to the spot, looking as though she'd flee if Adam weren't blocking her exit.

A chill trickled down Adam's spine.

His gaze tracked the room quickly. He saw two teacups and a half-finished breakfast on the table. An overturned chair lay across the room. A shotgun rested near a bent-willow rocking chair facing the window, and a woman's sneaker lay upturned in an odd position near the door.

The chill deepened.

"Where is she, Lydia?"

She swallowed, eyes flicking round the room. "I…don't know. She had a fight with Jett, just packed up all her bags and left in the truck," Lydia said quietly. "I came in to clean up."

She was lying. He could see it in her eyes.

Raw fear raked down Adam's throat as the horror of what might be happening dawned on him. He bent down and picked up the shoe. "Is this Muirinn's?"

"It must have fallen out of her bags. She left in a real hurry."

Adam limped over to the rocking chair, picked up the shotgun and checked it. It was loaded, a round chambered. He glanced at Lydia who remained frozen in place. "Did Chalky come get her?"

She said nothing.

"*Where,* Lydia! Where did they take her?"

"I don't know what you're talking about."

Adam cursed, gesturing at her with the gun. "If she dies, Lydia, *you* go down for murder!"

"And if you go after Chalky, we *all* go down. I know what happened in the mine, Adam," she said hoarsely. "You're in the same boat if this gets out."

"No," he said coldly. "I am not in the same boat. Because the difference, Lydia, is that *I* don't care if I go down now. I never intended to kill anyone twenty years ago, and I sure as hell have no intention of letting anyone else die now. This has to stop, even if it means turning myself in to the FBI."

He stormed out of the house, taking the gun with him. He tried again to call Jett from his Jeep. No answer. Lydia came rushing out the door after him, but Adam slammed the gearshift into reverse, hit the gas and shot like a wild man down the driveway, spinning backwards onto the dirt road in a spray of dirt and stones.

He raced for the airstrip.

If Jett was unaware of what had just happened to Muirinn, and he was not at home, there was one place he would be. His plane.

Sweat soaked his shirt as Adam drove faster, pain burning into his knees and hip. He hit Redial, steering with one hand, willing his son to pick up. Because there was no one else he could call. If Chalky had taken Muirinn, the Morans would be circling the wagons again.

That meant the police were the enemy.

The mayor was the enemy.

And there was no time to get FBI or state troopers in. He wasn't even sure there was still time to save Muirinn's life.

But he sure as hell was going to try.

Preparing for takeoff, Jett caught sight of his father, a pitiful figure hobbling fast over the tarmac, waving his hand high in the air. Jett started the engine, the prop of his Beaver turning over a few times then whizzing to a choppy blur. He opened the throttle and began to taxi out onto the runway.

But his father angled sharply across the field ahead, trying to cut him off. And as he neared, Jett saw the determination and grit on his father's face. And he a chill touched the base of his spine as he realized that Adam was carrying a shotgun.

He braked the plane and pushed back the sliding window.

"Muirinn's gone, Jett!" Adam yelled as he approached the plane. *"They took her!"*

He removed his earphones, hoping to God he'd heard wrong. "Where is Hamilton Brock? He was supposed to be guarding the house!"

Puzzled, his dad looked up. "No one else was there, except Lydia Wilkie. There were signs of a struggle inside the house, Jett. I think Chalky took her in his van—it wasn't at his house. If we can get up in the air fast, we might still see it."

Jett's stomach flipped over in dread. He quickly leaned over the passenger seat to swing open the door. "Get in!"

His father struggled to climb up, and Jett grasped his hand and helped haul Adam up. Their eyes locked for a second, tension simmering between them.

"Put the headset on," Jett snapped, as he turned to rev the de Havilland's engines. They took off into a brisk early morning headwind, and Jett noted that the distant bank of clouds to the west was closing in as he listened to his father relate how he'd rushed over to Chalky and Kate's place, found the van missing, saw the gun cabinet open and then raced to Mermaid's Cove.

"Lydia might even have given Muirinn some sedative or something because there were cups on the table, and she was trying to put everything away in a real hurry."

An image sifted suddenly into his mind—purple foxglove petals falling onto the back of Muirinn's hand as she left a note for Lydia Wilkie under the vase.

Gus could have been poisoned, Jett, a heart attack induced.

Had Lydia helped them with Gus, too?

Had she given Gus something—like digitalis tea made from foxglove—that had stopped his already damaged heart?

Jett's stomach lurched at the thought.

Could it have been Chalky who shot at Muirinn that day at the mine?

Jett recalled the ATV tracks that had headed up the mountain toward the eastern drainage. "Kate Lonsdale's family has always had land up north, up the eastern valley," Jett said coolly. "There's an old cabin on the property. They could be taking her there."

Reaching elevation, Jett dipped the de Havilland's wings sharply to the right, taking his craft out of the headwind and circling back. The dark bank of clouds to the west loomed closer, stray drops of rain beginning to fleck the windshield. The storm was moving in faster than had been forecast.

Jett flew up over the ridge and dropped low into the adjacent eastern valley, flying in a northerly direction as his father scanned the dirt road below with binoculars for signs of a vehicle.

Suddenly, through the trees, Adam caught the dust plumes of two vehicles racing north along the twisting track. He tapped Jett's arm and pointed.

Jett buzzed lower over the trees.

"Chalky's van!" his father said, scopes fixed on the column below. "And Gus's truck in front."

Panic whipped over Jett's chest and his hand tightened on the controls. He told himself he couldn't afford to panic. He *had* to stay focused if he was going to get Muirinn and her baby out of this alive.

He inhaled slowly, forcing his breath out in a slow, controlled fashion as his mind raced. The police were out of the question. He couldn't even call for SAR help—many of the SAR volunteers were tight with the Safe Harbor cops, and any radio chatter could be picked up. Jett didn't know who he could trust. He wasn't even sure now if he should have trusted Brock.

They had no choice—he and his father had to handle this on their own. And they had to be damn creative about it.

He shot his dad a glance. Adam's eyes met his, and a current of understanding passed between them. "We'll get her, son. I swear, we *will* get her." And Jett knew from the look in his dad's eyes, that despite everything in their past, they remained united on this one thing.

Jett nodded, and his father quickly went back to tracking the vehicles.

The dirt road below began to climb along the edge of a talus-filled canyon, and the trees thinned. Jett swooped down lower behind the vehicles, wings almost brushing the tips of the conifers.

But as he did, dust suddenly boiled out from behind the vehicles as the drivers sped up, realizing that they were being pursued by air. The van at the rear, without four-wheel drive, began to sway wildly on the steep dirt road, veering closer and closer to the cliff edge.

Jett's heart leapt to his throat.

Then the back doors of the van were flung open, and a body came tumbling out the back. It bounded hard on the dirt, all arms and legs as it rolled over the edge of the cliff and plunged down into the ravine, bouncing over rocks as it plummeted all the way down into the narrow crevice hundreds of feet below, until it disappeared into choking brush.

Jett's stomach lurched. "It's Brock," he whispered, praying that Muirinn was still alive inside the van.

Tilting the nose of his Beaver, he suddenly veered sharply up and over the next mountain.

"What are you doing?"

"They're going to have an accident and hurt Muirinn if we stay on them like that." Jett's face felt tight. "We have to assume that they're heading for the Lonsdale cabin. We can get there ahead of them."

"What if they second-guess us and turn back?"

Jett reached forward, switching radio channels. "There's only one road that leads north up the eastern drainage area, which means there is only one way out," he told his father. "We'll block the exit."

"How?"

"Like this." Jett radioed into the SAR dispatch. He said nothing about Muirinn or the Morans, only that he was in the air and had witnessed a man go down the mountainside. "He's hurt pretty bad, if he's even alive."

Grimly, he relayed the GPS coordinates indicating where Brock had fallen into the canyon. "You'll need to set the chopper down on the road. It's the only place to land," he said. "Get some guys to climb down, you'll find where he broke through brush and rolled over the edge. You're going to need ropes carabineers—full gear. I'll try to get out there as soon as I can get my bird landed," he lied.

By the time he signed off, the emergency chopper's rotors were spinning back at the helipad. The helo would be airborne and squatting smack in the middle of that exit road within minutes, followed hot quickly by ground ambulance and EMT personnel.

"If the Morans turn back now," he told his dad, "The road will be blocked." *With people who can help Muirinn.*

He flew low, following the course of the slow, meandering river in the eastern drainage, until his father pointed.

"There! That's the cabin. Down there in that grove of alders."

Jett began scanning farther along the river for a place to set his craft down.

Crouching in the dense alder and willow brush that surrounded the log cabin, Jett and his father waited for the vehicles to arrive. Between them they had a rifle, shotgun, two hunting knives, a can of bear spray, and several bear bangers—explosive cartridges that screwed onto pencil flares.

The minutes ticked by slowly. Rain began to come down heavily, and the sky grew dark and low with thunderclouds. The air felt hot, electric, in spite of the wind that rustled the tops of the conifers in the surrounding forest.

Suddenly, a plume of dust rose above the bush in the distance, and Gus's truck appeared. It pulled up in front the cabin and Kate Lonsdale jumped out. Face flushed, she rushed to the cabin door, hurriedly fumbling with keys to open it. She had a rifle slung over her shoulder.

Jett's pulse quickened. He placed his hand on his dad's arm, cautioning him to hold their position until the van arrived. "Wait until the driver gets out," Jett whispered. "Or we might risk them bolting. We'll never make it back to the plane in time, and we could lose her." His dad nodded, eyes fixed on Mayor Lonsdale opening the door.

Jett scanned the layout of the clearing, unsure of his plan. He wanted to get Muirinn away from them before they could get her inside the cabin, where they would be able to hole up with weapons.

A second plume of dust rose above the bush, blowing like spindrift in the increasing wind as the van approached.

Treetops were now beginning to sway with a soft hiss and

warm rain made his shirt cling to his body. Jett could sense the air pressure changing, too, a feeling of electricity in the air. They needed to hurry, or they might not be able to get the plane out again if the storm brought lightning.

He made a sign with his hand to show his father that he was going to sneak around to the far side of the cabin, where he could use the cover of vegetation to get closer to the door. There he might be able to head them off as they tried to carry Muirinn in.

He was just settling into his new hideaway when the van pulled up.

Jett's heart began to drum loudly in his ears, but ice-cool anger held him tight, fiercely focused.

Trees swayed violently. Heavy wind rushed through the trees now, cones and branches crashing down into the underbrush. Thunder rumbled in the distance. Not a good time to be in dry forest. Most fires out in the wild were sparked by lightning, and the effect could be devastating.

Chalky emerged from the driver's side of the van. Hurrying around to the back, he swung open the doors. Out jumped Bill Moran himself, still a strong hunter and outdoorsman in his early sixties. Bitterness leached into Jett's mouth at the sight of the old police chief.

It would've been Bill who'd thrown Brock out of the van.

Jett inched closer, peering through the leaves, wondering what his dad was thinking on the other side of the clearing. Adam Rutledge had as much—and more—to lose as the Morans did.

Could Jett trust him to pull through?

He *had* to.

Jett had to believe that the man he'd loved and respected and looked up to all these years was still inside that crippled body somewhere, and that he'd do the right thing when it came down to it.

The roar of the wind grew louder, and the sky darker. Lightning glimmered in purple clouds in the distance, followed by a rumble of thunder in the peaks. The rain came down in a sudden heavy sheet, releasing the musky scent of soil that had been dry for too long.

Chalky and Bill began to ease Muirinn out of the van, holding her up by the arms.

She's alive.

Jett's heart caught in his throat, and rage swelled in him.

She was gagged, bound, covered in dirt, her legs buckling out from under her as they tried to get her to stand.

Every molecule in his body screamed to blast out of the bush shooting wildly, but he forced himself to stay put. One wrong move could get them all killed.

Kate came back out the door, yanking a hood over her head as she ducked through the rain and ran toward the men, rifle in her hand.

Chalky moved away from Bill and Muirinn to shut the van doors, and Jett raised his weapon, sighting carefully down the barrel, Chalky in his crosshairs. He hooked his finger through the trigger guard, slowly put pressure on the trigger—then hesitated.

He'd never shot a man, and something deep in him resisted now.

It was wrong, in spite of what Chalky had done. This was not the way to end the secrets and lies and deaths of the past twenty years—it would be playing into the same game. Jett just couldn't do it. He would not allow Troy to one day look at him the way he'd been forced to look at his own father.

Instead, he slowly reached for the bear banger in the side pocket of his pants.

But before he could release the small trigger that would shoot the explosive cartridge out from the end of the pencil flare like a rocket, his father startled him by standing up suddenly and crashing out of the brush.

Everyone froze.

Kate was the first to react. She swung her rifle into position at her shoulder, aimed at Adam and pulled the trigger without a breath of hesitation. Almost simultaneously, Jett fired the banger.

It hissed from the flare, exploding like a grenade in a flash of light and sound behind Kate's head, sending her shot wild.

Kate dropped into a crouch, arms protecting her head as her rifle clattered to her feet.

Chalky ran toward his wife, thinking she'd been hit. He dropped to her side as Bill released Muirinn to lunge for his weapon in the back of the van. Muirinn crumpled to the dirt on all fours, and immediately started crawling for cover behind the van, drenched in rain and mud.

Bill swung his weapon into position and aimed at Adam. He pulled the trigger just as Adam blasted a slug from his shotgun.

Kate shrieked as a gaping hole tore through Bill Moran's chest and he was thrown backward against the white van. Chalky swung round, jaw slack, raw horror tearing across his face. *"Adam?"* he said in shock, still unaware that Jett was in the brush behind them. *"What in hell are you doing?"*

"It's over, Chalky," Adam's voice was thin, barely discernable over the beating rain as he raised his shotgun again. Wobbling slightly on his feet, he took aim at Chalky, who was still hunkered down, his arm around Kate. "The past ends right here. Drop your weapon."

Chalky slowly set his rifle on the ground at his side, his ghostly-blond hair slicking against his face with rain. "Adam, if *we* go down, you go down ten times worse," he said, desperation snaking through his voice. "*You* planted that bomb. *You* killed those men."

"And I will pay for it. We *all* will."

Jett reached for another banger, his body hot, humming with tension. Rain dripped into his eyes as he hurriedly screwed the cartridge onto the pencil flare, then fired.

The blast exploded right near Chalky and Kate's heads and they were momentarily stunned.

Jett used the instant to lunge forward, releasing a jet of bear spray on the pair huddled on the ground, incapacitating them further.

He coughed himself, eyes burning, rain drenching him, as he took their weapons and ran to the van. He grabbed a coil of wire from the back of the van. "Get Muirinn," he yelled to his father as he rushed back to Chalky and Kate. He bound them tightly, back to back, his mind racing.

Thunder clapped above them and rain drummed down even harder. Over the trees in deep purple clouds, white streak lightning stabbed down to earth with a violent crack. They had to get out, now, before one of those bolts started a wildfire. Even in heavy rain, flames could grow and roar like the wind.

Rushing around to the side of the van, Jett dropped to his knees, reaching for Muirinn who was huddled ghost-white on the ground behind the wheels of the van.

Where was his father?

"Jett!" she whispered, as she clutched him. "Thank God you came!"

He gathered her up, quickly checking her out. Her pupils

were dilated. And her pulse was thready. "Are you hurt anywhere?"

"No, just…drugged."

"What did they give you?"

"I don't know, but it seems to be wearing off."

"The baby?"

"She's still moving, I felt her kick." Muirinn glanced over his shoulder. "Jett, I'm okay. Your father—go to him!"

He whipped his head around. With shock he saw his dad splayed motionless, facedown on the ground, blood seeping out of a dark stain under him.

"He was hit, Jett. Bill got off a shot before he went down."

Jett scrambled over to his dad and rolled him over. Adam's head flopped back.

Lightning streaked from the sky again, cracking into trees a few yards away. Thunder boomed right over their heads. The wind roared, flinging debris at them from the trees.

Jett hunkered over his dad, protecting his face from flying twigs and cones, and his father's eyes flickered open. He was alive, breathing, but his dad had been shot in the gut, and the bleeding was bad. It was beginning to come out his mouth.

Muirinn shook Jett's shoulder. "Fire!" she said in an urgent whisper at his ear. "I can smell smoke."

Jett glanced back toward where the lightning had struck. Under the noise of the wind, he could hear the ominous crackle of flame taking hold in tinder-dry brush. He had to get Muirinn back to the plane, had to try to take off in this storm. Or they would die, consumed by fire in this desolate place.

He turned back to his dad. Adam's face was a cold, gray color that Jett knew well. Adam coughed up blood. "Go, son," he croaked. "Take her. Go. Start again."

"I can carry you, Dad—"

He shook his head slowly. "Go, please. I won't make it."

Jett hesitated. In the corner of his eye, he saw Chalky and Kate desperately pulling against their bonds, rain puddling around them.

Adam reached up suddenly, clutching at Jett's shirt. "It's better this way," he whispered. "I'd die in prison. And your mother would die just knowing I was in there. She didn't know about the bomb, Jett. This is right, the way it must be. Be...good to your mother. This...is..." His father went suddenly still, his hand flopping back down to the dirt as life left him.

Jett's eyes burned. Tears ran with the rain down his face. He felt Muirinn at his side again. He glanced up at her, anguish ripping through his chest. Her hair was plastered with rain to deathly pale cheeks, her eyes dark hollows.

His duty was with her now, with the baby.

His father had died to save the mother of his child—the daughter of the man he'd killed two decades ago.

But what about Chalky and Kate? He couldn't just leave them bound and incapacitated in the face of a fire. That was akin to murder.

Jett took note of the wind direction. If it held course, the fire would move to the east—it might even sweep past.

He cupped Muirinn's face in his hands. "The de Havilland is about a mile upstream. We can go along the bank. Do you think you can make it?"

She looked into his eyes. "We *have* to make it, Jett."

His father was right—the past had been put to rest, and he had to move forward, protect his woman, build a future. And if they made it out alive, he'd do anything, *everything,* to make sure they were together—her, him, Troy, the new baby girl. And his heart swelled with fierce energy.

"Start going to the river, Muirinn. Head upstream to the plane. Wait for me there."

"What about you!"

"Go! Now! I'm going to see if there's a radio in the cabin."

He hesitated for a split second, making sure Muirinn was moving toward the river, then he rushed into the Lonsdale cabin. He found the radio, set it to the right channel, and placed an emergency call to Search and Rescue, saying only that two people were injured at the Lonsdale cabin, and a fire was closing in. He had to yell as the storm played havoc with reception. "They'll be on the east side of Wolverine River! Downstream of the cabin!"

Thunder crashed again. A branch smashed down onto the roof. Jett signed off.

He'd call the FBI in Anchorage as soon as he got the plane down. If the SAR team didn't find them, an FBI manhunt would. There was nowhere for them to go, but into the wild.

Dashing out into the rain, he used his knife to cut Kate and Chalky loose, still dazed and disoriented. Holding a gun to their heads he said, *"Run!"*

They stared at him blankly, shivering, drenched. "Now! Or I'll shoot." He jerked the barrel of his rifle toward the trees. "Go that way, head for the river, downstream, cross it. I told the SAR guys you'd be there on the other side. Do it and you might escape the fire."

They took off, scrambling and stumbling into the bush as he fired into the dirt behind them for good measure.

Hands shaking as the aftereffects of the adrenaline dump took hold of his body, Jett raced after Muirinn.

They reached the plane, and Jett managed to take off into the sharp, gusty crosswinds. They flew into the deluge, water writing in pearly strings across the windscreen as they peered through the spinning prop blades.

Jett felt Muirinn's hand on his knee, and his eyes darted briefly to hers. And in that instant he knew that if he could bring her safely through this storm they would be able to finally bury the past, and find a way to a future. Together.

And nothing in this world would ever be able to tear them apart again.

Chapter 17

The past was finally being laid to rest—on all levels.

SAR crews had airlifted Kate Lonsdale and her husband, Chalky Moran, to safety, and they were now being held by the FBI for questioning in Anchorage, the town reeling from the news that their mayor and police department were implicated in the murders—from twenty years ago and today. Media crews had descended on Safe Harbor en masse, and towns-folk were finding solace in finally seeing their story told, the old wounds cleansed—and healed—for good.

The FBI had also taken Lydia Wilkie into custody. In an effort to lessen the charges against her, she had confessed her role in the case.

She'd told FBI investigators that just over a month ago she'd gone up to clean Gus's office while he'd stepped outside to smoke his pipe. Lydia had seen the "missing" crime scene photos of the Tolkin bombing on his desk, and she'd been unable to stop herself from reading what was on the screen of his laptop. That's when she knew that Chalky, her nephew and godson, was in serious trouble, along with his brothers. Lydia knew what had happened in the mine twenty years ago, and she was aware that it had been Don, then a rookie officer, who'd removed the crime scene photographs at his brother Bill's request. It was Bill and Don who'd then returned to the mine during the storm, and destroyed the tracks.

Lydia had gone straight to talk to her sister, Margaret, Chalky's mother. And the Morans had quietly closed ranks, asking Lydia to help them kill Gus.

Lydia said she was devastated by what she had to do, but she'd done it to save her family. She already knew what medication Gus was taking, and the small amount of dried foxglove leaves added to his comfrey tea, in combination with his medication, should have killed him, making it look like a natural progression of his illness.

However, Gus had been impatient to get to the mine that morning and had barely touched his tea. The toxin had thus not worked right away, and Gus had driven out to the mine.

In desperation, she had phoned Chalky, and in a panic, Chalky and Kate had headed out to the mine where—just as Trapper Joe had indicated—Gus was feeling ill, and succumbing to digitalis poisoning. They made him climb down the shaft, where his heart had finally stopped.

They'd then driven his truck home.

However, when news of Gus's absence finally hit the papers, someone passing by on a hunting trip remembered having seen Gus at the mine. And that's when the search dogs were brought in. But upon locating the body, Don was able to persuade the ME and Dr. Callaghan that there was nothing suspect about how they'd found Gus.

Lydia had also been the one who'd removed the laptop from the table drawer, and she'd administered a sedative in Muirinn's tea, but not enough to kill her—the Morans had wanted her alive so that they could use her to lure Jett.

Hamilton Brock had not been so fortunate. He'd been shot and killed with a police-issue handgun.

Jett would never forgive himself for leading Brock into mortal danger. His buddy had no idea what he'd been dealing with. Even he hadn't grasped the sheer gravity of the situation at the time. But the main thing was that he'd flown through that storm, and he'd landed Muirinn and her baby safely.

Go, son. Take her. Go. Start again.

His father was right. Adam had given his life to atone for the sins of the past, and it was now time to move forward—in Adam's memory. In Troy O'Donnell's memory. In honor of all those who'd died and suffered because of the tragedy.

Jett entered the hospital room just as Dr. Callaghan was completing Muirinn's ultrasound.

He'd had Troy fetched home, and the boy was sitting in the waiting area. Jett had spoken to his son, telling him everything.

Muirinn smiled as Jett neared her bed. "Dr. Callaghan says everything looks good."

The doctor looked up as she covered Muirinn's tummy with the sheet. "Everything seems okay, Jett. There's no evidence of anything at all in Muirinn's bloodstream. Whatever Lydia Wilkie administered worked through her system very quickly. The baby would have felt similar woozy effects, but the good news is that we're into the third trimester, everything is fully formed and her vital signs are all good." She smiled warmly, hazel eyes twinkling. "Mother and daughter are going to be just fine."

Jett stole a glance at the image still up on the ultrasound monitor, and his heart contracted so tightly at the sight of the blurred human form that he felt tears burn. He reached for Muirinn's hand, looked into her amazing green eyes, into the lost years. And he didn't need to say the words—they were finally sharing what they'd missed the first time around.

A pregnancy.

He smiled, throat thick with emotion. "I have someone I want you to meet."

Her face changed, anxiety creeping into her green eyes. "He's *here?*"

Jett nodded. "I had him flown back. We need to be together now." He paused. "I've told him, Muirinn. I've told him that you're his mother."

Muirinn's heart began to patter, nerves dampening her palms. She moved up into a sitting position, her entire being focused on that doorway.

Troy appeared—the dark-haired boy she'd seen on the dock. In the photos. Jett's son.

Her son.

He hesitated in the doorway, glancing up at his father. Jett nodded encouragement, and Troy stepped into the room. His hair was the exact same inky-black as Jett's, his skin tanned. Big green eyes fixed on her—the same unusual moss-green as her own eyes.

"Troy," she said, her voice coming out soft and strange to her own ears. She felt so afraid. So fragile...so worried she'd scare him away.

Silently, he walked up to her bedside, his gaze riveted on her, his little mind processing so much.

He was clearly not a shy child—his walk showed a young confidence, a latent curiosity. And Muirinn loved Jett even more for being a good father, a father who could foster and nurture this sort of character in his son. It was the kind of confidence that would serve him well in life. Yet apprehension showed in his eyes, in the way he fisted his hands at his sides.

Muirinn ached to hold him, squeeze him so tight, grab back all the childhood that had been lost to her.

"I've heard so much about you, Troy."

Troy nodded, silent.

"Jett told me you're named after my father."

"He died before I was born." His voice brought tears into her eyes. Her son. A second chance…it was overwhelming. The tears spilled over and ran down her cheeks. She laughed nervously, reaching for a tissue to wipe them away.

"My dad said Troy O'Donnell taught him about planes, and that's why my dad is a pilot."

Muirinn tried to swallow around the incredible emotion balling painfully in her throat. She nodded. "He…he was your grandfather."

Troy nodded all too sagely for his years. Warming easily to the conversation in between glances at his dad for reassurance. "I know. My dad told me. And that makes Gus my great-grandfather."

"What did your dad tell you about me?"

Troy shot another glance at his father. But Jett stood quietly to the side, letting his son direct things where he needed them to go. Troy turned back to Muirinn.

"He said he always loved you, and that you are my mom. But that you couldn't be here right away. That you needed time."

Muirinn was unable to talk. She looked at Jett, his gaze held hers.

Then little Troy's mouth flattened, and he drew a breath in

deep, as if he were mustering courage. He glanced at Muirinn's tummy, then down at his shoes, then up again. "Can I touch it?"

"The baby?"

He nodded fiercely.

"Yes," whispered Muirinn, taking his hand, her heart breaking at the sensation of it in her own. She placed the little palm on her belly, on top of the covers. "If you wait you might feel her move."

He narrowed his eyes, focusing intently, a boy raised here, in wild country, open about life and death. The way she liked it. The way Muirinn wanted it to be.

"There," she whispered. "Did you feel that?"

His green eyes flared, and his mouth dropped open. "Was that the *baby?*"

"Yes." She smiled. "That was your sister."

"Cool!" He grinned, a bright white slash of teeth against his tanned skin. All kid again. The kid she'd glimpsed at the dock, the child she'd envied Jett for having with all her being. The child she had not known was hers.

Jett stepped up, placing his hand on his son's shoulder. "The nurse outside has ice cream for you, Troy. I need a word with Muirinn, and then she needs some rest."

Troy grinned at her, bounded out.

Muirinn didn't trust herself to speak for several long minutes. "Thank you, Jett, thank you so much. He…he's…" Tears streamed again, and she couldn't talk at all. Jett took her into his arms. "It'll take a while," she said between sniffles into his shoulder. "I'm just so happy to be able to watch him grow."

"You really are going to stay?"

She'd told him over and over again, but Jett was almost afraid to believe it, to accept that, this time, it really might happen.

"I wouldn't leave for the world, Jett. Everything that is precious to me is right here in Safe Harbor."

He stood silent, energy raging like wildfire through him. Why in hell was he so scared?

Because he really didn't want to screw up this second chance.

Then he came right out and said it—not the way he'd planned, but because he was terrified he'd miss the opportunity. "Marry me, Muirinn. I don't want secrets, I don't want boundaries." He hesitated, suddenly panicking that she'd say no. "I just want you. I always have."

She stared at him in silence, and Jett felt perspiration prickle over him. "We can finally be a family, Muirinn," he said, voice rough with emotion. "The way it should have been."

She inhaled deeply. "I've wanted nothing more, Jett," she whispered.

"Is that a yes?"

She nodded, tears flowing down her cheeks. "All these years..." she swallowed, wiping her eyes. "I...I never dreamed I could have a second chance."

And he gathered her into his arms, and kissed her. Never again would he let her go. This time she was here to stay.

December.

Muirinn stepped up and placed a twelfth long-stemmed white rose alongside the eleven others on the small cairn of mining rocks. On top of the cairn rested a miner's hat with a headlamp.

She lowered her head and said a silent prayer for her father, for her mother, for the families of all the men who had lost their lives that tragic day. And she prayed for Adam Rutledge, and for Hamilton Brock.

For the future.

For the sins of all fathers to be forgiven.

Then, solemnly, she returned to her pew in the tiny church where her family stood.

Jett slipped her hand into his. He was holding Arielle, her two-month-old daughter, bundled up warm in his arms.

He and Troy had helped name her—after a mermaid. From Mermaid's Cove. In honor of Gus, who had once made Muirinn believe that she, too, had been brought up from the sea.

Muirinn closed her eyes as voices rose in hymn, and she said a special prayer for her grandfather. But she didn't need to. Because she felt him here, watching over them, just as she felt the tiny bone compass warming against her chest. Gus had shown her a way home.

He'd shown her true north.

It was snowing softly when they left the church, having finally laid the miners' memories to rest. The town could now move forward, and the future had started with winter snows blowing in over the sea.

Jett put his arm around Muirinn, drawing her close. Arielle was tucked in under his jacket, warm as a bun, and Troy ran ahead, jumping into new snowdrifts, Christmas lights twinkling in the town.

Jett's chest swelled with fierce devotion, happiness, and he leaned down and kissed his bride-to-be.

She smiled up at him, snowflakes like white confetti dusting her red curls.

It was these simple pleasures, thought Jett, that made it all worthwhile, and the fresh snow was redolent with promise of a long winter. A time of rebirth.

Because in the spring, they would marry, and it would all be new again.

And he couldn't be more happy. He had his family at last.

"I'm going to finish her," he said suddenly, as they walked trough the drifts, arm in arm.

"Finish what?" her voice was dreamy, soft.

"*Muirinn of the Wind.* I'll do it over the winter, give her wings. She'll be ready to fly by summer."

Muirinn looked up into her man's deep-cobalt eyes. "I love you, Jett. I always have."

"I know," he whispered.

She laughed, and he kissed her softly on the mouth, thinking of the tune that had been playing on his truck radio when he'd driven past Gus's house and first glimpsed that light up in the attic.

I believe in miracles.

And today, he did.

* * * * *

Don't miss THE SHEIK'S COMMAND,
The first book in Loreth Anne White's thrilling
new miniseries SAHARA KINGS.
Coming to Silhouette Romantic Suspense in 2010.

*Celebrate 60 years of pure reading pleasure
with Harlequin®!*

To commemorate the event, Silhouette Special Edition
invites you to Ashley O'Ballivan's bed-and-breakfast in
the small town of Stone Creek. The beautiful innkeeper
will have her hands full caring for her old flame Jack
McCall. He's on the run and recovering from a mysteri-
ous illness, but that won't stop him from trying to win
Ashley back.

*Enjoy an exclusive glimpse of Linda Lael Miller's
AT HOME IN STONE CREEK
Available in November 2009 from
Silhouette Special Edition®*

The helicopter swung abruptly sideways in a dizzying arch, setting Jack McCall's fever-ravaged brain spinning.

His friend's voice sounded tinny, coming through the earphones. "You belong in a hospital," he said. "Not some backwater bed-and-breakfast."

All Jack really knew about the virus raging through his system was that it wasn't contagious, and there was no known treatment for it besides a lot of rest and quiet. "I don't like hospitals," he responded, hoping he sounded like his normal self. "They're full of sick people."

Vince Griffin chuckled but it was a dry sound, rough at the edges. "What's in Stone Creek, Arizona?" he asked. "Besides a whole lot of nothin'?"

Ashley O'Ballivan was in Stone Creek, and she was a whole lot of somethin', but Jack had neither the strength nor the inclination to explain. After the way he'd ducked out six months before, he didn't expect a welcome, knew he didn't deserve one. But Ashley, being Ashley, would take him in whatever her misgivings.

He had to get to Ashley; he'd be all right.

He closed his eyes, letting the fever swallow him.

There was no telling how much time had passed when he became aware of the chopper blades slowing overhead. Dimly, he saw the private ambulance waiting on the airfield outside of Stone Creek; it seemed that twilight had descended.

Jack sighed with relief. His clothes felt clammy against his flesh. His teeth began to chatter as two figures unloaded a gurney from the back of the ambulance and waited for the blades to stop.

"Great," Vince remarked, unsnapping his seat belt. "Those two look like volunteers, not real EMTs."

The chopper bounced sickeningly on its runners, and Vince, with a shake of his head, pushed open his door and jumped to the ground, head down.

Jack waited, wondering if he'd be able to stand on his own. After fumbling unsuccessfully with the buckle on his seat belt, he decided not.

When it was safe the EMTs approached, following Vince, who opened Jack's door.

His old friend Tanner Quinn stepped around Vince, his grin not quite reaching his eyes.

"You look like hell warmed over," he told Jack cheerfully.

"Since when are you an EMT?" Jack retorted.

Tanner reached in, wedged a shoulder under Jack's right arm and hauled him out of the chopper. His knees immediately buckled, and Vince stepped up, supporting him on the other side.

"In a place like Stone Creek," Tanner replied, "everybody helps out."

They reached the wheeled gurney, and Jack found himself on his back.

Tanner and the second man strapped him down, a process that brought back a few bad memories.

"Is there even a hospital in this place?" Vince asked irritably from somewhere in the night.

"There's a pretty good clinic over in Indian Rock," Tanner answered easily, "and it isn't far to Flagstaff." He paused to help his buddy hoist Jack and the gurney into the back of the ambulance. "You're in good hands, Jack. My wife is the best veterinarian in the state."

Jack laughed raggedly at that.

Vince muttered a curse.

Tanner climbed into the back beside him, perched on some kind of fold-down seat. The other man shut the doors.

"You in any pain?" Tanner said as his partner climbed into the driver's seat and started the engine.

"No." Jack looked up at his oldest and closest friend and wished he'd listened to Vince. Ever since he'd come down with the virus—a week after snatching a five-year-old girl back from her non-custodial parent, a small-time Colombian drug dealer—he hadn't been able to think about anyone or anything but Ashley. When he *could* think, anyway.

Now, in one of the first clearheaded moments he'd experienced since checking himself out of Bethesda the day before, he realized he might be making a major mistake. Not by facing Ashley—he owed her that much and a lot more. No, he could be putting her in danger, putting Tanner and his daughter and his pregnant wife in danger, too.

"I shouldn't have come here," he said, keeping his voice low.

Tanner shook his head, his jaw clamped down hard as though he was irritated by Jack's statement.

"This is where you belong," Tanner insisted. "If you'd had sense enough to know that six months ago, old buddy, when you bailed on Ashley without so much as a fare-thee-well, you wouldn't be in this mess."

Ashley. The name had run through his mind a million times in those six months, but hearing somebody say it out loud was like having a fist close around his insides and squeeze hard.

Jack couldn't speak.

Tanner didn't press for further conversation.

The ambulance bumped over country roads, finally hitting smooth blacktop.

"Here we are," Tanner said. "Ashley's place."

* * * * *

*Will Jack be able to
patch things up with Ashley, or will his past
put the woman he loves in harm's way?
Find out in
AT HOME IN STONE CREEK
by Linda Lael Miller
Available November 2009 from
Silhouette Special Edition®*

This November,
Silhouette Special Edition®
brings you

NEW YORK TIMES
BESTSELLING AUTHOR

LINDA LAEL MILLER

At Home in
Stone Creek

Available in November
wherever books are sold.

REQUEST YOUR FREE BOOKS!

2 FREE NOVELS PLUS 2 FREE GIFTS!

Silhouette® Romantic

SUSPENSE

Sparked by Danger, Fueled by Passion!

YES! Please send me 2 FREE Silhouette® Romantic Suspense novels and my 2 FREE gifts (gifts are worth about $10). After receiving them, if I don't wish to receive any more books, I can return the shipping statement marked "cancel." If I don't cancel, I will receive 4 brand-new novels every month and be billed just $4.24 per book in the U.S. or $4.99 per book in Canada. That's a savings of at least 15% off the cover price! It's quite a bargain! Shipping and handling is just 50¢ per book*. I understand that accepting the 2 free books and gifts places me under no obligation to buy anything. I can always return a shipment and cancel at any time. Even if I never buy another book from Silhouette, the two free books and gifts are mine to keep forever.

240 SDN EYL4 340 SDN EYMG

Name _____ (PLEASE PRINT) _____

Address _____ Apt. # _____

City _____ State/Prov. _____ Zip/Postal Code _____

Signature (if under 18, a parent or guardian must sign) _____

Mail to the **Silhouette Reader Service:**
IN U.S.A.: P.O. Box 1867, Buffalo, NY 14240-1867
IN CANADA: P.O. Box 609, Fort Erie, Ontario L2A 5X3

Not valid to current subscribers of Silhouette Romantic Suspense books.

Want to try two free books from another line?
Call 1-800-873-8635 or visit www.morefreebooks.com.

* Terms and prices subject to change without notice. Prices do not include applicable taxes. Sales tax applicable in N.Y. Canadian residents will be charged applicable provincial taxes and GST. Offer not valid in Quebec. This offer is limited to one order per household. All orders subject to approval. Credit or debit balances in a customer's account(s) may be offset by any other outstanding balance owed by or to the customer. Please allow 4 to 6 weeks for delivery. Offer available while quantities last.

Your Privacy: Silhouette is committed to protecting your privacy. Our Privacy Policy is available online at www.eHarlequin.com or upon request from the Reader Service. From time to time we make our lists of customers available to reputable third parties who may have a product or service of interest to you. If you would prefer we not share your name and address, please check here. ☐

SRS09R

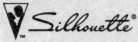

Silhouette®

Romantic
SUSPENSE

**Sparked by Danger,
Fueled by Passion.**

---

*Blackout
At Christmas*

Beth Cornelison,
Sharron McClellan,
Jennifer Morey

What happens when a major blackout shuts
down the entire Western seaboard on Christmas
Eve? Follow stories of danger, intrigue and
romance as three women learn to trust their
instincts to survive and open their hearts to the
love that unexpectedly comes their way.

*Available November
wherever books are sold.*

Visit Silhouette Books at www.eHarlequin.com

SRS27653

Silhouette® Romantic SUSPENSE

COMING NEXT MONTH

Available October 27, 2009

#1583 BLACKOUT AT CHRISTMAS
"Stranded with the Bridesmaid" by Beth Cornelison
"Santa Under Cover" by Sharron McClellan
"Kiss Me on Christmas" by Jennifer Morey
In these short stories, three couples find themselves stranded in a city-wide blackout during a Christmas Eve blizzard.

#1584 THE COWBODY'S SECRET TWINS—Carla Cassidy
Top Secret Deliveries
All Henry Randolf wants for Christmas is to be left alone. But Melissa Morgan shows up at his Texas ranch with adorable twin boys— quite clearly *his* twin boys—and he knows his life will never be the same. When a crazed killer puts the new family in his sights, Henry and Melissa must learn to work together—for their love and for the safety of their boys.

#1585 HIS WANTED WOMAN—Linda Turner
The O'Reilly Brothers
As a special agent, Patrick O'Reilly always has to put duty before desire. But his current suspect, Mackenzie Sloan, is tempting him beyond belief. Her eyes assert her innocence, though the evidence is against her. Will Patrick decide to trust his head…or his heart?

#1586 IMMINENT AFFAIR—Sheri WhiteFeather
Warrior Society
The first time warrior Daniel Deer Runner met Allie Whirlwind, he was injured saving her life. Now there are gaps in Daniel's memory— a memory that includes falling in love with Allie. But when Allie's in danger again, he's hell-bent on protecting her. Will their old feelings resurface before time runs out?

SRSCNMBPA1009